Dear Reader,

As a child, I used to listen in fascination while my grand-father told stories. I would marvel at his expression and passion. And then when I went to bed, my parents would take turns telling me bedtime stories. The journeys I went on in my imagination were beautiful, but what I loved most about these stories were the messages behind them.

So when I wrote *Hope* I wanted to tell a story with a message. A story that doesn't underplay how hard life can be, but that also doesn't underestimate how hope can inspire the will to go on. Most of all, I wanted to share a story about my home, Zimbabwe.

I grew up knowing that Zimbabwe was the breadbasket of Africa and it broke my heart when so many things changed. But the part that is rarely told is this: even though it was a time when people could have easily been broken, the resilience I witnessed was astounding. I saw a hope that I pray will remain alive and usher us to better times.

This is a book inspired by what really happened. A story about a place I love. I hope that as you read it you'll get angry, you'll laugh, you'll be shocked and perhaps even cry at times. But I hope you remember through all that emotion that hope is our only wing!

—Rutendo Tavengerwei

HOPE
IS
OUR
ONLY
WING

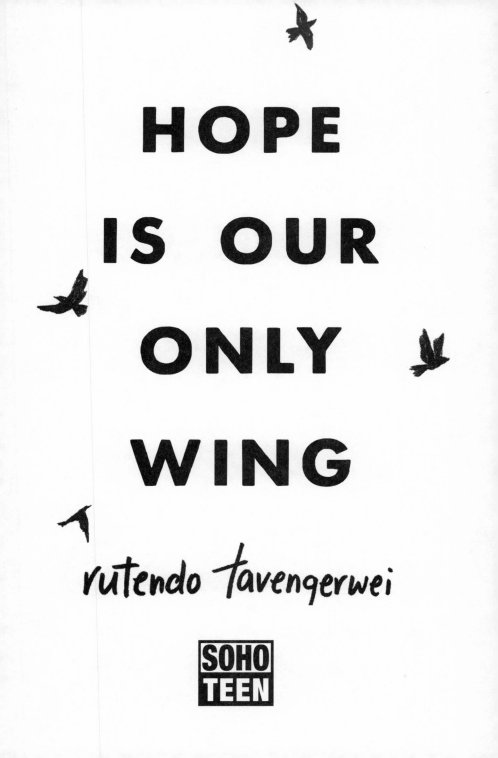

HOPE IS OUR ONLY WING

rutendo tavengerwei

SOHO
TEEN

Published in the United States by Soho Teen
an imprint of Soho Press, Inc.
853 Broadway
New York, NY 10003

Library of Congress Cataloging-in-Publication Data

Tavengerwei, Rutendo
Hope is our only wing / Rutendo Tavengerwei.

ISBN 978-1-64129-072-2
eISBN 978-1-64129-073-9

1. Friendship—Fiction. 2. Grief—Fiction. 3. Sick—Fiction.
4. Boarding schools—Fiction. 5. Schools—Fiction. 6. Political corruption—Fiction.
7. Zimbabwe—Fiction.
PZ7.1.T3838 Hop 2019 [Fic]—dc23 2019000820

Interior design by Janine Agro, Soho Press, Inc.

Printed in the United States of America

10 9 8 7 6 5 4 3 2 1

For my lovely parents, Simbarashe and Jenifer Tavengerwei.
Thank you, among so many other things, for introducing me to
the world of writing and storytelling.

PART ONE
January 2008

1

Shamiso's heart broke into a shudder of beats. She could hear the jazzy trails of the mbira spiraling in the air. Her father would have loved that sound. She glanced at her mother, who stood next to her, fanning her sweaty neck. She seemed preoccupied. The music played on, painful and familiar.

When Shamiso was eight, her father had insisted that she learn how to play. The metal pellets had bruised the tips of her fingers as she plunked on them. A series of confused notes bumping into a glorious discord. The frustration had been too much for an eight-year-old, made worse by the fact that none of the other kids at school understood quite what the instrument was.

Shamiso listened as the voice of the mbira rose proudly. Whoever was playing knew what they were doing. She could hear the underlying tone of a hum that flowed well with the song. And in that magnificent noise floated all the memories and feelings she was trying to ignore.

Her mother hovered by her side, trying to figure out where they should go. Shamiso felt numb, staring down at her shiny new shoes and listening to the music that disturbed the air.

"Shamiso." Her mother hesitated. "Are you all right?"

"I told you before," Shamiso muttered, biting her breath, "I don't want to be at boarding school. Especially here!"

She watched her mother wipe her damp neck as though she had not heard her. Her blouse clung to her skin, moist from the sweat.

"There's no time to cry," her mother said softly. "Wipe your tears, mwanangu. You'll be fine." She nodded at the administration block in front of them.

Shamiso saw the exhaustion on her mother's face as they picked up the luggage and headed for the building. They sat in the waiting room and looked around. The young man behind the reception desk seemed caught up in a tsunami of phone calls. The walls were lined with pictures of alumni at different events across the years. Shamiso could hear snatches of conversation from two men standing by the door.

"Yes, but by staying away . . . we . . . are only punishing the children," one of the men said rather slowly. Shamiso kept her head down, concentrating on the tracks of the mbira.

"You are beginning to sound like that journalist . . ." the other man commented.

Shamiso raised her head. She guessed the men were teachers, but she could barely hear what they were saying. She leaned in.

"Of course . . . we . . . we have to be smart about this," the first man continued, his voice rising in volume.

A bubble of anger formed in Shamiso's throat. She tried to keep calm. Her ears picked up the music, which was slowly forming into a song. She wondered if she would ever be able to play like that.

The notes poked at her brain. Her father had called it the sound of home, the stolen guitar of nature. She closed her eyes. Memories sat vividly in her mind. His fingers dancing around on the little pellet strings, his lips pursed, the music swirling. She held her breath, scared that if she breathed out too soon she would lose him.

A sudden voice jolted her back to the present. "Aww, first day at school, is it?"

Shamiso opened her eyes and wiped them with the back of her hand. A girl stood in front of her, holding a pile of books. Her curly hair was tied back tightly into a bun. She seemed to be headed for the staffroom.

"Newcomer or first form?" the girl asked.

"I'm new," Shamiso mumbled.

"Would you look at that! We have ourselves a Brit," the girl declared.

Shamiso gritted her teeth. The door to the staffroom suddenly opened. The cartoon on the door warned her that it was out of bounds. A teacher stood in the entrance, blocking the view as though the staffroom was some sacred destination that students were not meant to see. All Shamiso could hear was laughter as the teacher beckoned the girl inside.

"Well, don't worry, Your Majesty, it will definitely get worse. The queen doesn't come here for tea, I'm afraid," the girl said in her best imitation of what she thought was an English accent before following the teacher inside.

Shamiso fought the urge to call after her. She had hardly been in this country long and she was already certain she did not like it at all.

2

Shamiso stood beside the plump principal. Her mother had left—not that Shamiso had wanted her to stay. The principal signaled for the class to sit down.

Shamiso fidgeted. Her armpits stung and fear jeered right in her face. The last time she had been in a new place, her father was there. Things had always fallen into place when her father was in charge. She pulled the cuffs of her cardigan into her palms and held them tight.

"Good morning, class," the principal's hadeda voice rang out.

She looked over the students, poised like a goddess standing with her hands sharply by her sides, her spectacles beneath her cold eyes. Her navy-blue dress perfectly matched the seriousness of her face. Her thin, curly, gray hair lay tired on her head. She seemed as though she was probably no more than a year or two from being bald.

"Now, I have Miss Muloy with me. She is new and will be joining us this term. I would like to stress that here at Oakwood we pride ourselves on our hospitality."

She paused for effect. Her spectacles slid down to the tip of her nose as she placed a hand on Shamiso's shoulder.

"There's an empty seat at the back; you can make your way there."

Shamiso did not want to be here. She turned slightly toward the principal and could see it in her eyes that she knew this too. Still, Shamiso did what she had been asked. Her fists swung close to her hips and her breath was tempered. She glanced at the rest of the students, each with a book opened on their desks as though someone had taken the time to carefully align them. Their shirts were a crisp white, with the girls in green cardigans and the boys in maroon.

The room itself was old, with sagging paint and aging Post-its, windows with rusty frames and the wood-tiled floor.

She stared at the tiles. There was something about their tired and unkempt state that she could relate to.

"You can sit down!" the principal told her, but it was as if Shamiso wasn't in her body. She continued to stand, almost dazed, her feet forming some sort of bond with the floor.

"To sit, or not to sit, that is the question." One of the students chuckled. The class broke into wild sniggers as Shamiso snapped back to reality.

"Quiet!" the principal said, turning to one of the girls at the front. "Paida, shouldn't you be keeping the class in check until your teacher arrives?" Shamiso's eyes popped. The girl! The girl from reception! She shifted toward the principal.

"Because of the strike, ma'am, Miss Ndlovu hasn't been coming to teach us. We were reading from our Shakespeare set book. I believe that's what Tinotenda is referring to," the girl said with a smirk on her face.

The principal halted by the door. "Things are hard for the

staff, but I will talk to Miss Ndlovu." She paused. Three distinct lines formed on her forehead. "Paida, can I trust you to make sure that Miss Muloy settles in?"

"Yes, ma'am!" the girl answered confidently.

As soon as the principal was a safe distance away, the class broke into chatter. There was only one thing Shamiso liked about this arrangement: she could sit in the back corner where she could hide and blend into the wall. She opened her desk, fighting the lump in her throat. She had to pull herself together. Her mother had insisted on this school. She was convinced that it was only at a mission school that a good education was guaranteed, and she had groped for every cent she could find to pay the fees.

Oakwood High was one of the few mission schools left in the country, built by missionaries during the unstable liberation war of colonial times. It was located close to Chinhoyi, just a few kilometers west of the capital Harare. It had stood there for decades, thriving due to its exceptional pass rate and good morals.

Traveling to Oakwood had been close to a nightmare. Since petrol was scarce, only a few buses a day went to Chinhoyi. The bus had been packed beyond capacity in spite of the heat. Shamiso leaned close to the classroom window, still sticky and hungry for fresh air. She wiped the film of sweat from her forehead and gazed at the enormous oak tree outside. It reminded her of home.

"You know, it's always a good idea to come a day early. It takes away most of the stress and frustration," the student in front of her said, turning around. She had a delicate voice, soft like ripples of water, and a smile that lit up like gasoline. She extended her hand.

9

Shamiso lowered the lid of her desk, her eyes gliding from the girl's face to her outstretched arm. The girl's eyes had bags under them, carrying a world of fatigue. Shamiso stared a second longer and looked away. She could make out a mbira beneath the girl's chair. She blinked rapidly, reached for her backpack and felt for her textbook.

"Around here, you're going to need friends," the girl said with a chuckle. "When you realize that, my name is Tanyaradzwa."

3

Shamiso's mother sat on the bus on her way back home. She knew her daughter hated the new place. To be honest, she hated it too. But she had to keep it together if they were to make it through this. She stared outside, watching the trees rush past. Shamiso's tuition would cripple her finances. But at least the new environment would keep her daughter distracted for a while. She fanned her face with one hand. The last time she had ridden down this road was when her husband had taken her to see the famous Chinhoyi caves. He had asked to marry her that day. She smiled as she remembered how nervous he had been the whole drive there. It hardly felt real.

She wondered if this was one of the many times he had gone chasing a story. Memories crowded in, and she shook them off. There were more important things to do. She had to figure out how she would take care of her daughter; how she would get money. All this had caught her off guard! But time is friend to no man. The cuddling eventually stops and time's blow unleashes its rage.

4

A series of screeches spread across the room as the chairs scraped against the classroom tiles, the students all scrambling to their feet. Everyone except Shamiso, who remained seated.

A short middle-aged man stood in front of the class, one hand holding a textbook and the other stroking his carefully trimmed beard. She could hardly make out his face. He paused awhile before placing the book on the mahogany table in front, then began to walk between the rows of students, inspecting the classroom with lazy eyes. As he got closer to Shamiso, she sensed an uneasy recognition. She had seen him earlier in the administration block, though he had not seen her.

Tanyaradzwa glanced back at her, eyes raised, begging Shamiso to get up. Shamiso knew she ought to stand, but something stubborn hardened inside her.

The man walked on, one hand in his pocket, his steps calculated as though preparing to pounce on an unsuspecting chicken. His knees refused to bend, making him drag his feet as he walked.

As he neared her seat Shamiso sprang up, avoiding eye

contact. He stood by her side, his breath touching the soft skin of her face.

"Mmm," he murmured. "Please don't stand up on my account." There was a pause. "Your name?"

His exaggerated pauses aggravated Shamiso. He seemed to enunciate every word, taking his time, like someone combing lice out of a child's hair. She turned to him. He wore a proud smirk, ready to assert his power. She noticed little spurts of sweat on his face and felt pleasure in knowing that the heat was baking him to perfection in his elegant coffee-colored suit.

"Umm . . . Shamiso. Shamiso Muloy," she said, her trimmed accent causing waves of amusement in the class. Tinotenda softly mimicked her until the teacher glanced back with a stern look. He stared at Shamiso for a second longer as though he recognized her from somewhere, then turned and began walking toward the front of the class.

"And you are . . . ?" Shamiso asked.

He halted. The class brimmed with whispers, nervous on her behalf.

"Excuse me?" he said.

"You are?" she repeated, holding her voice so it wouldn't tremble.

The teacher drew closer, pushing his face into her space. He lifted his left eyebrow a little. She drew her head back.

The class stared at her, some in awe, others in plain amusement, waiting to see what would happen next.

"Why do I hear noise?" he breathed, tilting his head and turning to the group of girls nearest to him. There was immediate silence.

He turned back to face Shamiso. His right hand was in his pocket, and his left fidgeted with a piece of chalk.

"Looks as if we will have fun here, won't we?" He signaled to the class to sit down, then paused, tugging at his chin hairs. "But maybe *you* shouldn't sit down."

Shamiso froze.

"You know . . . so that your brain will retain my name . . . like mine has yours. It's Mr. Mpofu . . . Don't worry . . . I guarantee . . . you definitely won't be forgetting it."

He stared at Shamiso, as if to make sure a cold chill ran down her spine. Shamiso turned and looked out of the window next to her. Her heart beat wildly as she stood there, listening to his voice echoing in the room.

"Now, class, we are going to be looking at equations today," he said, flipping through his textbook. "There is an example on the first page. You know what to do." Mr. Mpofu stared into his book, his head close to the paper.

Shamiso turned to him. "Excuse me, I'm not clear on these instructions," she blurted out, a wobble of fear. She looked around the class. Wonderful. She had become quite the spectacle.

"Mmm, well, if most of you get it right, then I'll allow you to proceed with today's exercise."

He selected a piece of chalk and scribbled something on the board, his speed at odds with his personality.

Shamiso weighed up the numbers and symbols carefully. "Excuse me . . ." she said hesitantly. "I think you got that wrong."

"What did you say?" he asked, lifting his head from the textbook.

"The equation's wrong. There is a bracket there, so you were supposed to multiply first, before you divide."

"Oh . . . so you think you are a genius?" he said, inspecting the board to verify his answer.

He stared at the board a bit longer, then looked at Shamiso, his eyes digging into her flesh. Without another word, he erased the answer and wrote in a new one. Whispers surfaced everywhere. The teacher twisted to face the class, narrowed his eyes then turned back to the chalkboard.

"Try solving this . . . since you are such a genius," he said, writing a new problem.

Shamiso chewed on her pencil and stared back at him with a blank face.

"Our friend here . . . is challenged. What is wrong now?"

Shamiso popped her knuckles one by one, her eyes fixed on him. "The answer is 38b."

He looked at her for some time, then flipped to the back pages of the book with urgent speed. He glanced again at the chalkboard and then went to the answer in the textbook. A wry smile came over his face. He clapped his hands then stopped. One clap . . . another . . . and another, dramatic and slow.

"I'm impressed. Have you done this before . . . at your previous school?"

"No." A slight smile crept up on her, stretching the corners of her lips. "I woke up like this."

The room broke into laughter. Mr. Mpofu reached for his beard again and paced slowly in front of the class. "Without the attitude . . . maybe you'll go far." He nodded. "Now, class . . . today's work is on the board. I want my answer booklets in . . . Bring them to the staff office . . . first thing tomorrow morning. And the whole chapter for our maths genius here . . . That will be sixty-eight equations to solve."

Shamiso began to protest, then, seeing the look on his face, retreated. She took on the challenge.

5

The siren sounded, ending the first leg of the day's lessons. Lunchtime! Students scurried off to the dining hall, a short distance away.

"You still think you can do this alone?" Tanyaradzwa asked.

Shamiso disregarded her completely.

Tanyaradzwa shrugged. "Suit yourself." She fastened the buckles on her backpack before making her way out of the room.

Shamiso waited till Tanyaradzwa was out of the door then followed the masses, walking down the wide avenue rich with arching jacaranda and gum trees swaying blissfully on the sidewalk. She breathed in the thick scent. A lump formed in her throat. Her father would always talk of the old festival that happened when the jacarandas were celebrating the birth of November. This was back in the day, after the liberation war, when her father had been only a boy growing up in the village, with a growing patriotism and booming zeal to serve his newly born nation. Back when the country had just transitioned from Rhodesia to Zimbabwe.

Her father would tell stories of the war, the "guerrilla struggle." He would talk of how the country had been won back from colonial rule by the revolutionaries. He had wanted to be part of it, to fight for his country, for the freedom of his people. The issue for him was that he had been too young then. But when he had grown older, living in the city, he had tried to serve his country in his own way: with his writing. She remembered his heartfelt oration of his newspaper article about how the liberation struggle had changed everything.

The gentle breeze from the trees accompanied her as she walked alone to the dining hall. She wiped her brow again. It had been a long time ago and she had been very little, but she did not remember it being this hot. She looked up into the clear blue sky, so different from the gray skies that usually loomed over Slough.

Her friends back there had asked her before she left if she would be living with tigers and elephants in the jungle, like Tarzan. She hardly remembered life back in Zimbabwe, but she had still found it strange that they would ask that. She smiled as she thought of it. All she could do was pray that distance would not be ill-mannered and greedy. That it would not swallow up her friends, tire their efforts and erode all the memories.

She missed her friends back in Slough, especially Mary-Allen and Katlyn, and the times she used to stroll over just to hang out with them. Now all that depended on time difference, school schedules and a significant phone bill she could hardly afford. Even so, it was hard not to feel hurt that they hadn't made more effort, especially knowing what had happened to her. But this was why she didn't need friends. Because in the end, one way or another . . . everyone leaves.

Her shadow flickered in front of her, a reminder of her loneliness. She sensed endless prying eyes skittering in her direction and picked up her pace, eager to reach the dining area. The circling spotlight zoomed in. All the laughter and giggles seemed directed at her.

She finally made it to the dining hall. The tiles on the roof had been scorched by the heat. Its contrast with the vibrant color of the trees was unbecoming.

A young man sat on an old bench under the shade of one of the trees. His overalls were rolled up, leaving his lean ashy legs exposed. He was possibly from the nearby farm. A matchstick was parked at the corner of his mouth, swinging gently at the tickle of his tongue. A watering can sat by his foot. His eyes moved in Shamiso's direction. She wondered if he had watered anything at all. The lawn lay thirsty in the sun, patchy and dry.

"This way," Tanyaradzwa said, signaling Shamiso to follow her. Shamiso looked at her in surprise. Tanyaradzwa beckoned again, so Shamiso followed her to a table in the middle of the dining hall. Every table had two bowls, each covered by a plate to keep flying things out. Next to the bowls sat a pile of ten plates, two ladles and a pile of spoons.

Tanyaradzwa slid into her chair. "It's bean soup if you're wondering." She lifted the plate covering one of the bowls. Shamiso straightened her face and drew out a chair. A thick aroma escaped from the bowl. Tanyaradzwa chuckled as she noticed Shamiso's expression.

"They used to make really good food, to be fair," Tanyaradzwa said as she fidgeted with the plate, sliding it back into position. "It's just that lately . . ." She stopped herself.

"Oh, you'll get used to this . . . or you could always do the more acceptable thing: starve!"

A smile escaped Shamiso's lips. She quickly tucked it in and looked away. Something about these peeling walls reminded her of the little cottage she had left her mother in back in Rhodesville, a low-density suburb in Harare. It seemed nothing could be done about them there either. Her mother had tried, insisting that the cottage should feel like home. She had scrubbed the walls until her nails bled. But because the paint was white-wash, that had only discolored the walls even more. Shamiso wondered as she sat there what she resented more—being stuck in a boarding school in the middle of nowhere or those awful dining-hall walls.

She glanced again at the peeling paint. Definitely the walls.

6

The sun danced in the light blue sky, showing off its rays. The heat teased the students as they walked to their hostels after a tiring day. The directions that Shamiso had been given led to a red-brick walled building inside the hostel complex. It looked newer than the others, as if it had been recently erected.

Shamiso dragged her luggage along the corridor. Her satchel rested loosely on her shoulder. It had been a difficult first day. She had never been to boarding school before. Her father had worked for a small political newspaper and certainly did not make enough money to afford to send her to boarding school in England; not that she'd minded.

There was an incredible energy in the chitchatting students that stretched beyond her reach. They ignored her, as though she was invisible. The attention she had been so worried about seemed to have fizzled away; perhaps the heat had dried it up. The weather wasn't as she remembered it. She had thought the rains would escort the old year out in December and usher in the new year in January. But everything was different because of the drought. It didn't rain as much anymore, and the heat ate away at everything! It was a shame about the weather.

Opening week felt strangely relaxed. She could see students busying about, catching up with one another, laughing in little groups and tidying their rooms.

"Are you lost?" a passing girl asked Shamiso with a quick smile. She was a bit older, and her uniform was different from the others. Rather than a green cardigan, hers was white, and instead of a flared skirt, she wore a pencil one. She held a clipboard to her chest and a pen in her left hand. Her presence intimidated Shamiso.

"Who are you?" Shamiso asked curiously.

The girl crossed her hands. "Are you lost? Yes or no?" The smile had vanished now. She stood waiting for a reply.

"Neither. I just need to find my room."

"Well, you won't find it with that attitude. What's your name?"

"Shamiso Muloy," she answered.

The girl paused awhile, flipping through her clipboard. "I'm a prefect," she said eventually. "This way." She stopped near the end of the hallway and stepped back to allow Shamiso to enter before scribbling something down. "I hope next time we meet the attitude will be gone," she said, not looking up. "Oh, and if you're going to survive here, you definitely want to respect your prefects. Definitely!"

Shamiso drew her head back. Surely this wasn't like the movies with some domineering authority they all had to obey. Maybe the prefect was joking?

She offered a tentative smile. "Yeah . . . whatever?"

The prefect looked at her with her face buttoned up, shook her head and walked away.

Shamiso stood just inside the doorway, luggage held lightly in her hand. The room carried a rich aroma of floor polish. She could see the floor gleaming in the light from the wide window at the far end. The room lay empty, with just a few traces of human existence. Trunks sat adjacent to some of the beds. One or two buckets stood abandoned. She entered slowly, eyes darting around. Two of the beds had already been made. A third had its bedding simply put on top, and the fourth, in the corner of the room, was untouched. She walked to the empty bed, realizing that it now belonged to her, hauling her suitcase before dumping it in front of the bed. She reached for the handle of the window and pushed, but the stiffness of the paint still held it. She struggled awhile before finally giving in.

As she sat, trying to get used to this place that was meant to be her new home, she felt a painful lump in her throat. Tears streamed down her cheeks before she could control them. Hearing the sound of footsteps getting closer, she wiped her wet cheeks, knelt beside her bed and opened her suitcase. There was barely anything in it. Her mother had only been able to part with a little money. She had bought a few things so she could have some snacks to munch on through the course of the term. But then again there was barely anything in the stores anymore. There had been nothing much to buy, except a few packets of maputi and biscuits.

"Well, look at this!" a soft voice said a few seconds later. It was Tanyaradzwa, with two carefully ironed shirts hanging neatly from her arm.

She caught her eye for a tiny moment before turning back to her unpacking.

7

Shamiso lay on her bed, shivering slightly. She fought the urge to go outside and peered out from the corner of her blanket to see what Tanyaradzwa was doing. She seemed to be reading something, a Bible perhaps.

"Are you all right?" Tanyaradzwa whispered.

Shamiso froze, her body tense. She held her breath, waiting for Tanyaradzwa to ask again. The lump slipped back into her throat. She quietly reached under her pillow and felt for a small object. "I need some air," she explained, slipping out of the room before Tanyaradzwa could say anything else.

The corridor carried a looming darkness. All the lights had been switched off and only a few hisses and giggles floated in the air. Shamiso followed the corridor, then scurried through the open door.

The moon was out and its light paraded on the pitch-black walls. A slight undercurrent of crickets created a background tone. She looked around. There was no life whatsoever. Her heart thudded, pressing against the cage of her chest. She walked to the side of the building and retreated into a corner.

She leaned her back against the prickly grains sticking out of the brick wall.

She could feel the tears swelling. The darkness had a familiarity she recognized. Her whole body ached, and parts of her itched. She pulled out a little box from her pajama pocket. She had to make the pain disappear somehow. She pressed her hands to her eyes, wiping away the tears. Little threads of moisture were beginning to form in her nose.

Slowly, she slid her back down the wall, until she was sitting down. She closed her eyes as the brick grazed her skin. She sat on the concrete with her knees drawn up and her head lodged in between them. She could taste salt from the traces of tears that ran past her lips.

She pulled her toes against the ground, pressing them hard onto the stones that showed in the concrete. The rough pebbles tore her skin.

She opened the little box. They were all there, the six white rods of the cigarettes she had placed inside.

She lit one and brought the cigarette to her lips, watching the smoke as it came out of her mouth. The feeling of the smoke seemed to heal her insides. She tapped the cigarette and smiled as pieces of ash fell to the ground and thoughts of her father crept through her mind. She brushed her toes on that rough concrete again. Her hands moved to her head, holding it tightly as a stream of tears unleashed the rage stored up inside her. She could not stop them, and for the first time she did not try to.

8

Tanyaradzwa sat alone and awake, listening to the whistles and snores of her roommates.

She could see traces of moonlight through the small crack in the curtain. She wasn't sure she could cope with another night of insomnia and heavy thoughts. Fatigue haunted her lately, always around this time. There wasn't much she could do, except lie in bed and wait for sleep to come. She turned to face the other way. As she lay there breathing, someone gently opened the door. She watched through the thin cloth as the new girl limped in. There seemed to be a pain troubling her feet.

Tanyaradzwa wondered why she was trying to befriend this mysterious girl who clearly did not want anything to do with her. Tanyaradzwa had managed to keep all her relations at bay, making sure no one got close enough to discover her secret. She had successfully reduced the time she spent with her old friends by hiding herself in books. It helped that they had been put in different classes and hostels.

But there was something about Shamiso. Something that ignited an inexplicable wave of pity in her. As she puzzled over this strange emotion, her eyes began to close and eventually she drifted into the rest of the night.

9

Shamiso rubbed sleep from her eyes, feeling the sunlight creep in through the window. She had been awake all night, fighting nightmares.

She listened to Tinotenda, who sat on the teacher's table reading the day's news out loud. It was almost midday now. None of the teachers had made it to class. Mr. Mpofu had left a copy of the morning paper, insisting that they were to be kept updated on what was happening.

A handful of students drooled, sleeping on their desks while others played cards. Only a few engaged in a rich exchange of opinions on the upcoming elections. The election date had just been announced. The prevailing feelings were fear and hope. There seemed to be a good representation of both. Shamiso listened in, intrigued how anyone could be certain that a change in political power would mean a change in everything else.

"If it wasn't for the illegal sanctions, my dad says the country wouldn't be in such turmoil," Paida said, her voice dominating the conversation. There followed hisses of disagreement, wrapped in caution because it was a sensitive subject, tricky to be so open about. Shamiso shook her head. She had heard about it on the news: the EU and the US had imposed sanctions on the government after the land grab.

"It's true! There's barely anything that the government can do, you know! Their hands are tied!" Paida continued, determined to defend her point of view.

"Bollocks!" Shamiso scoffed, shepherding the conversation in an interesting direction. Everyone sat quiet, their eyes dancing between her and Paida. The boys sitting next to Paida burst out laughing.

Shamiso frowned and looked out of the window. The thin, crunchy twigs of the oak tree caught her attention. The tree seemed parched, stripped of all life. The wind rustled, snapping a few twigs. Shamiso turned back to Paida, whose face was twisted in annoyance.

"What do you know about Zimbabwean politics, London girl?" she hissed. She seemed to be taking it personally.

Shamiso smiled. It was a strange insult when she wasn't even from London. "More than you for sure. I know I don't believe that the country is in a shambles because of sanctions!"

An uncomfortable silence fell over the class.

"You want to be careful what you say, and where you say it, London girl," Paida shot at her.

"You need to learn to keep your mouth shut sometimes," Tanyaradzwa whispered softly.

There was something that did not add up. She understood that the subject was touchy, but surely in a class of teens there was no one to be afraid of? A nervous energy fluttered in the room.

"Did anyone hear about that journalist who died?" Tinotenda suddenly spoke up, holding the paper in his hand.
Shamiso's heart lurched.

"The papers are saying his death is suspicious, as he was
trying to expose the government. It's still being investigated,"
he went on.

Shamiso's eyes darted around, watching to see if anyone
would say anything. The class remained silent.

"What was his name again?" Paida asked.

"I don't know his real name," Tinotenda said, flipping the
other pages of the paper. "They keep referring to him by his
pseudonym. Out of respect for his family or something like
that."

"Oh, I think I've heard about him. The one who got
deported from the UK because he had been working on some
dodgy plot against the government, right?" said Paida.

Shamiso flinched. Where had all these fabrications come
from?

"He was a troublemaker, writing lies and working with
the West. His death wasn't suspicious. Didn't he have an accident or something?" Paida continued.

Shamiso tried desperately to calm the rage rising within her,
but it spilled over, bigger and more powerful than she was.

"You really are full of it!" she blurted out, gritting her
teeth and breathing heavily.

Tanyaradzwa looked at her in concern.

"What did you say to me?" Paida asked, getting to her
feet.

The class suddenly went quiet. Paida quickly sat down.
Shamiso turned to the door. Mr. Mpofu stood in the doorway, leaning on the frame, lips pursed, stroking his orderly

chin hairs with his left hand. His right hand balanced a cane on the crooked tiles of the floor.

"Why do I hear noise?" he whispered. He turned to Paida.

She glanced at Shamiso and smirked. "Sir, we were trying to do the work you gave us yesterday, but the new girl created disruptions and that's what caused the noise," she said, her voice rich with confidence.

"That's a load of—" Shamiso began to protest.

"I didn't ask you . . . to . . . defend yourself," he said lazily, swinging the cane like a pendulum. He stood there for a little longer, stingy with his words, drenching the class in suspense. Then his finger signaled for Shamiso to follow him.

As she headed to the front of the classroom, her eyes met Paida's. It sat there in her look. The war had officially begun.

10

Shamiso's eyes followed the cane in Mr. Mpofu's hand as it swung back and forth. Her left hand was clenched into a tight fist. Shame and rage buzzed around her.

"You've not been here long . . . and you're already making trouble?"

She avoided his gaze in silence, all the words she would have wanted to use stuck in her throat. He gave his swinging cane a rest and placed his hand in his pocket.

"Come," he beckoned, heading into the staffroom. She hesitated for a moment, wondering if he was testing her. The first thing she had seen when she had arrived at this school was that the staffroom was out of bounds for students. The little cartoon stuck by the door would not let her forget it!

She followed him inside and looked around the room in bewilderment. There were more teachers in there than she had expected. A few of the chairs were unoccupied, but most held teachers who were sitting at tables reading or marking scripts. Two or three hovered by the kettle, holding mugs of tea and engaging in conversation. None of them seemed to be in a hurry to get to class.

"Muloy . . ." Mr. Mpofu summoned her from her day-dreaming. She hurried toward him as he dug around in the messy order that was his desk, piled with newspaper articles and all sorts of books.

"Channel your energy . . . into something worthwhile," Mr. Mpofu advised, handing her a thick textbook. His brow furrowed as though he was thinking of something important. "Have the first chapter . . . on my desk by tomorrow morning."

Shamiso flipped through the book as she scanned to see how many equations he expected her to solve. Her eyes flickered in shock.

"Sir, it's more than twenty pages!" she protested.

"Would you like more?" His face faked bemusement.

Shamiso grunted.

"Didn't I say . . . you won't be forgetting . . . my name?" he reminded her.

Shamiso walked back to class. She still wasn't sure that she liked him, but to her surprise, a grudging respect showed its head and promised to come out at full light.

11

Mr. Mpofu sat in his chair, eyes drooped, watching the girl as she walked out of the staffroom. He could tell that something had broken within her and he knew what it was. He had wanted to tell her of the day he met her father. The day her father had inspired him with his determination and hope for the future of the country. How infectious his energy had been. He had wanted to tell her that she resembled him.

But the murmurs he had heard floating around with her father's name made him nervous. His political views were slowly entangling him in a spider's web. How could he pull her into that world? He sighed and held his head in his hands, reminding himself that it was for the girl's own good.

12

The hostel was quiet when Shamiso returned later that day. The wind whistled in the hallway, and a few doors swung in tune. There was no sign of life. Everyone else was at the afternoon's sporting activities.

Shamiso lay on her bed, facing the ceiling and listening to her heartbeat.

Somehow she couldn't stop thinking about her father. She remembered how they would lie outside in the dark, looking at the stars. He always insisted that it released his creative juices and allowed them to run wild. There wasn't much inspiration in the ceiling now—only old paint and a dangling dusty bulb.

The stubborn lump in her throat slid back, scraping and wiggling itself into comfort. Her eyes fought a stream of uninvited tears. She sat up and opened her suitcase, marveling at the sight of the laughing face next to her father's, framed in time and posted on a photograph. She had stuck it to the inside of her trunk to remind her. And there, in the corner, was her precious pile of newspaper cuttings. Her hands ran over the top one and she pulled her father's satchel close. She wanted him there with her.

She unzipped the front pocket and a yellow envelope slid out. Her father's writing danced across the top of it. She could see the ink was smudged, as though he had written it in a hurry. Her heart stood still for a second, her eyes scanning the writing on the envelope in hope that he had left it for her.

Her eyes hovered over the name and address, someone called Jeremiah. She had never heard of him. The lump slid back into her throat, mocking her with thoughts of how all the pieces of her father that remained were related to his work. Just like all those boxes surrounding her mother in their little cottage. Neither Shamiso nor her mother had been able to face sorting through them.

"What are you doing here?" A panting voice came out of the blue.

Shamiso pushed the envelope back into the satchel. "Heavens! You made me jump!"

Shamiso watched Tanyaradzwa drag herself across the room and onto her bed, which was next to Shamiso's. Her gasps for air made it clear that she was desperately short of breath.

Shamiso's hand brushed over her wet eyes and she shifted her loot of paper next to her.

"You aren't supposed to be here, you know," Tanyaradzwa spoke again, still trying to catch her breath.

"You're here!" Shamiso objected.

"I'm allowed!" Tanyaradzwa smiled.

"Are you okay? You don't look too good."

Tanyaradzwa lay quiet for a while, then spoke softly. "You have an English accent?" She caught sight of the inside of Shamiso's trunk and smiled at the picture of father and daughter.

"Yeah, I lived there with my family since I was five."

Tanyaradzwa sat up slowly, resting against the wall.

"Why did you come back to Zimbabwe then?" she asked.

Shamiso swallowed hard. She picked up the papers and stared at them again. Her right hand shook slightly, sending tremors through the little pile of cuttings.

Tanyaradzwa leaned closer, eager to make out what was written. Her eyes ran over the columnist's name and back to the photograph stuck to the inside of the trunk. And just like that, her heart skipped a beat.

PART TWO

Three weeks earlier

13

Tanyaradzwa lingered by the door, almost frozen, staring at the memories of the last time she had been here. But she told herself today was a good day, in fact one of the very best.

"Please come in. I've been expecting you," the doctor said, holding the door open with the weight of her back and wiping the spectacles in her hand. Tanyaradzwa skipped into the room, her mother following right behind her. The doctor watched as mother and daughter giggled over something they had been talking about in the waiting room.

The lights in the corridor flickered. The electricity threatened to turn itself off. The doctor frowned. The room was hot, and powering the building by generator was too expensive. The electricity would have to behave. After all, she would need it if it would be possible at all to save Tanyaradzwa's life . . .

The doctor closed the door and walked to her chair. There weren't many oncologists in the country anymore. The rich pool of talent had diminished, scattered across the globe in search of greener pastures. The few that were still available came at a hefty price.

Mother and daughter sat in the cushioned chairs. The papers on the doctor's desk flapped in the breeze. Tanyaradzwa leaned closer to the fan, enjoying the feeling as it ruffled her short Afro.

The doctor, a light-skinned elderly woman with speckled gray hair, fumbled with the papers on her disorganized desk.

"You look like you have been busy," Tanyaradzwa began. The doctor nodded, explaining to them how hectic her week had been, with this conference to go to, and that place to be. A stack of papers fell to the floor as she shuffled everything around. Tanyaradzwa peeped at the newspaper on top.

The doctor blinked. "It's a shame about that journalist, isn't it?" she commented, placing the papers back on her desk.

"Ahh, chokwadi, death is a thing to behold. It seems like only yesterday when he was reporting on the Campbell land-grab case! And now he's gone," Tanyaradzwa's mother responded.

The doctor cleared her throat. Some things could not be spoken about so openly.

Tanyaradzwa fidgeted, unwilling to engage in a conversation about politics. Excitement teemed inside her like a purring kettle. This visit marked the official start of her remission. The doctor had assured her of that the last time she had seen her.

"How's band practice going, Tanyaradzwa?" the doctor asked as she pulled the chair with its creaking wheels closer to the desk.

"Oh, I forgot to tell you—we've been asked to perform at the music festival again this year. I'm quite excited. I actually have practice today," she fizzed.

The doctor smiled. "I hope I'm invited. After last year's

performance, I don't think I can ever enjoy hearing anyone else sing besides you."

Silence crept in for a moment. The doctor scribbled something on her pad. Tanyaradzwa made no effort to read it. After all, everyone knows that doctors spend a full year of med school learning how to write illegibly, as though creating a secret code. Tanyaradzwa looked around the room. The poster of the human heart still hung there on the wall close to the door.

The doctor rested her elbows on the desk, holding her hands close to her mouth. Slowly, she lifted her head and looked Tanyaradzwa right in the eye. "I'm afraid I don't have good news."

Tanyaradzwa glanced at her mother, confusion swirling around her. Her legs stopped swinging.

The doctor peered at her from behind her thick bottle-carved spectacles. "Are you eating, Tanyaradzwa?" she asked suddenly.

Tanyaradzwa's brow furrowed. What did that have to do with anything? She looked again at her mother, who was staring steadily at the wall. No emotion leaked from her face. She seemed to already know where this was going.

The doctor sighed. "The tests show that the cancer is back."

"But . . ." Tanyaradzwa began. "But you said—you said once I was in remission, you said . . . you said I was fine!"

The doctor swallowed. "I know, and I'm sorry. The cancer seems to be rather aggressive."

Tanyaradzwa's mother brought her head down. Her elbow rested on the chair's arm and her nose sat in the face of her palm. Tanyaradzwa sat, expressionless, staring at the doctor.

"Am I going to die then?" she blurted out. The doctor hesitated. Tanyaradzwa picked up the flicker in her eye. It was impossible to miss.

"Like I said, the cancer is aggressive," she replied. There was no easy way to deliver such news. She propped herself up. Her voice became softer, her determination stronger. Her hands rested neatly one on top of the other.

"This time there is a very small tumor growing on your vocal cords and wrapped around one of the major nerves in your throat. We can operate on the tumor now, but I'm afraid it is very risky, given where it is located. If we are not careful, then you might end up losing your voice . . . or worse."

Tanyaradzwa scratched her nose. "Then I guess you'll have to be careful?" She blinked with feigned innocence.

The doctor swallowed. "I'm hoping that how we did it last time will work again now. So I'm going to recommend chemo and radiation, possibly in higher doses. I mean, the tumor is small enough for this to be a possibility." She shifted position. "Are you planning to change schools?"

"No!"

"Yes," her mother said at the same time.

The doctor took a deep breath. "We can have you taking something to keep the tumor from growing."

Tanyaradzwa watched as the doctor's lips moved. She could hear nothing. The noise of her thoughts drowned the doctor's voice. Her mind wandered, fear infecting her thoughts and doubts blooming. This morning she had woken up with the hope of a new beginning. But now the bubble had burst. Her reality had changed in the blink of an eye.

14

The wind carried Grandmother's words through the window to Shamiso as she lay in bed, a voice—one that Shamiso barely recognized—that now carried colorful stories of a younger version of her father.

"Then when my granddaughter Shamiso was born, there were complications. But just like her father, she's a little fighter, that one. And he was so determined that she would make it. He would carry her on his back and tell her about the war as though he had been there." The audience laughed. Shamiso remembered the many times her father had narrated the story of her birth. She had loved hearing the part where he had to be begged for visitors to be allowed to hold the baby. "He was always quite the storyteller. Even when he was only a boy, when we told folktales around the fire, he would always volunteer and his stories would never end . . ."

She listened as her grandmother attempted to make the audience laugh again. It was what her father would have wanted. He had always been one to make jokes.

Now she could hear singing coming from outside. There were a few distinct wailings; probably from her grandmother, whom she only really knew from the photograph her father had kept in his wallet. He had never spoken about her. Shamiso had been aware of the money he sent to his mother, but that was about it. It was strange that their only connection had been a bank account number. Now she was in this woman's house, in her bed, mourning her son.

The last time she had been to her grandmother's farm, she had been a toddler, back before they had moved abroad. She hadn't even remembered the banana trees lining the entrance. She wondered if they would have made this trip at all had her father not died. Or if her grandmother had not insisted that he should be laid to rest on his father's land and not in some cemetery in the city.

She watched as speckles of dust danced in the light coming through the window. They held her attention for a moment, spiraling toward her as the door opened. Her eyes immediately slammed shut. She could hear footsteps quietly approaching.

"Shamiso," she heard as she was gently shaken. "You need to eat, mwanangu." It was her mother's voice.

She cringed. The soft hands resting upon her hurt. Her mother's frame, close to her on the bed, hurt. Her mother hurt. Shamiso lay there in silence, unable to move.

"Shamiso," her mother tried again. "They are going to let us view the body soon." She took her hands off Shamiso's back. The bed rocked softly. Shamiso could still feel her presence there. She opened her eyes and turned to face her. Her mother's hands were pressed over her mouth, cupped as though muffling screams. Shamiso watched the stream of tears that rolled down her hands, past her nose and through the spaces between her fingers.

Shamiso felt it too, whatever it was. The whole world was collapsing. The walls that had held it together were giving in.

15

The last time, there had been something sitting in her neck. She had not known it for a while and had suffered for her ignorance. When the doctor had finally detected it, Tanyaradzwa had to muddle her way through a series of radiation sessions. They had taken her hair, a bit of her weight and a few friends. Tanyaradzwa remembered the pity she had received from those who tried to be supportive; and how she had resented it. She had moved schools to start afresh. And two years at Oakwood had allowed her to keep a careful distance. No one knew who she was or what she had been through.

But even through all that, the cancer had not messed with her voice. Tanyaradzwa fidgeted at the prospect of the work the band had to do in preparation for the upcoming music festival. She glanced at her phone to check the time. The car turned off the Robert Mugabe Road into Glenara.

"Mama, I am meeting the guys for practice, remember?"

Her mother kept driving for a while, then answered, "You have to rest, Tanyaradzwa."

Tanyaradzwa could see the stress that colored her mother's brow. The cancer sat proudly in between them, third-wheeling. Tanyaradzwa could only imagine the distress all this was causing her parents. Surviving it once was enough. Twice would be a show of just how fragile the human spirit was.

Tanyaradzwa broke into a soft song. Usually her mother would join in; it was their "thing" when they drove together. But today her mother kept her eyes on the road and Tanyaradzwa eventually brought the song to rest.

She focused on the view outside the window as the car moved past the trees in Tongogara Street. The clouds floated in the sky, forming and re-forming into moving shapes. The sky was blue. Her world was exploding, but the sky was still blue.

Her gaze shifted to the people in the street. They were a collection of stories, every one of them part of the grand narrative of how things were. When the car stopped at the lights her eyes rested on two men selling airtime on the corner. They were in the middle of what looked like an entertaining conversation. She marveled at their carefree laughter.

The traffic light changed to green and they carried on. A black Mercedes drove side by side with them. The contrast was stark. There on the corner were the men selling airtime, while this young man in his early twenties drove his big car and wore an expensive suit.

All this thinking drained her energy. She turned to her mother. Her eyes were bloodshot and damp with tears. Tanyaradzwa looked away. There had to be hope; at least one of them had to have a speck of it. It was the voices she had to fight, the voices screaming for her to give in.

She had to fight them. She had to try.

16

Shamiso listened to the singing as she stared at her father's suitcases, heaped on top of each other in the corner of the house. He had always carried a suitcase and a satchel when he traveled. Her gaze lingered on the satchel thrown on top of the cases. He barely left home without it, but had almost forgotten it when he was leaving the UK this time around. She remembered the panic as he was leaving, worried he would miss his flight, yet laughing and teasing her mother for her unease. He had been excited about this story he was chasing, though he never told them the details of his investigations until they were complete.

The singing started to trade with the sun. The softer the heat got, the louder the singing became. Funerals in the rural areas were so different from city ones. Actually, she had not been to many at all. She had only been to one in the UK: a teacher's. There had been no singing, just silent sobbing and a lot of polite nibbling.

Things happened differently here. A group of men and women sang and danced, totally consumed with song, not only in celebration of the deceased's life but also in a bid to distract their loved ones from the pain of their loss. It had even worked on her for a minute or two.

The crowd outside continued fattening. She could hear murmurs of conversation. After all, her father had been well known because of his work. He had tried to champion hope. It seemed a lot of people had appreciated his writing.

She had come here by car with her mother and her uncles. They had driven by Christmas Pass, allowing them to see the enchanting array of Mutare's sparkling lights, a city built in a valley and guarded by mountains all around. It had been like something from a postcard. She knew her father would have made them stop to enjoy the lights if he'd been there, but it would have been odd to do that now. Especially with all these other people coming to the funeral, driving with them in a long procession of cars making their way from Harare to her grandmother's little farm in the hilly plains of Vumba.

The drum outside voiced a distinct thump, its rhythm drifting into an echo. As it pounded louder and louder, she could feel her heart synchronizing to the beat, thudding in sequence.

"Shamiso, it's time," she heard. Her pulse began to race. She was not ready. It was the thought of seeing her father confined within the boards of that damning wooden box that scared her. And the reality that it would be the last time she would look at him.

He would no longer make pancakes in the morning. She would never again hear him read his work aloud, trying to make sense of it. Her heart sank. She knew she had to go; she had to see him, to say goodbye.

Shamiso made it out of the farmhouse, the sun shining

right onto her face. The crowd had grown larger since she had last seen them. There were cars everywhere. People stood against the walls of the farmhouse, women on one side and men on the other. She could see her mother by another door, almost unresponsive. Her eyes were glazed and her face blank, leaning against the newly thatched hut, rocking herself back and forth.

Two women rushed to Shamiso and dragged her into their embrace, sobbing dramatically at the same time. She stood there, struggling for breath, held tightly in their arms.

"That dress doesn't quite do for a funeral, mainini," one of the women whispered, sending an unwelcome splatter into her ear. She looked at them in confusion. The music stopped. The women moved slightly aside, still weeping. Somehow she had become the center of attention.

As she tried to make her way over to where her mother was, she saw three men exiting the hut with her father's coffin. Her legs gave way, just as screams and wails erupted from everywhere.

17

The cushion was beginning to lose its fluff. Tanyaradzwa had sat on it too often and now the wood of the window ledge was digging into her. But even so, she preferred the discomfort of the ledge to being in bed.

Her eyes wandered to the beautiful mbira sitting proudly on her display table, between the two music trophies. The auburn wood glimmered as she dragged herself over and lifted it. For such a light object, it felt heavy. She took it to the window and began to play. The melody filled the room. Her thumbs tapped at the keys of the hollow instrument. It moaned, sending notes of music flying all around her. Her shoulders swayed slowly to the tune. Her voice joined in the harmony, humming softly in a deep undertone. She closed her eyes and allowed the music to soothe her.

The sky roared in agreement. She stopped playing and glanced out of the window, placing the mbira down beside her. The clouds were darkening and spiraling. Swallows danced in the sky, forming a beautiful sequence. It had always been said that the swallows beckoned the rains. She watched their parade. It had not rained in a long time.

Dark clouds were hovering, pushing the sun away. A loud clap of thunder sounded. Tanyaradzwa rubbed the goose-bumps on her arm and glanced down, just in time to see the gardener getting ready to push his wheelbarrow full of tools back to the wooden shed in the corner of the yard. She watched as he stared up at the clouds. There was hope in his stance, hope that the rains would fall. She could see it. Somehow, that hope coincided with hers.

The door opened without warning. She turned to see her mother carrying a tray.

"You know, this load-shedding is really getting out of hand. They sent another notice saying we won't have electricity for three hours this time. Can you imagine?" Her mother ranted in frustration.

Tanyaradzwa was only half listening. She knew maintenance costs for the electricity plants were skyrocketing, burdening the government's resources. ZESA had just announced on the news that some of its generators in Kariba were faulty. Parts of the country would have to tolerate load-shedding while they tried to fix them. Everyone was adjusting.

Her mother's voice softened as she drew closer. "You have to take your medicine and rest."

Tanyaradzwa looked at her mother's puffy face. She could see how strong she was trying to be.

The food tickled Tanyaradzwa's nostrils. She held her breath. Her appetite had deserted her and the smell was too aggressive. She took one more peek at the clouds and climbed off the ledge onto her bed.

Her mother helped prop her pillows so she would be

comfortable and brought a spoon of soup toward Tanyaradz-wa's lips. The aroma was too much. She could feel the saliva pooling in her mouth, and suddenly, there it was! Her insides ached as, yet again, she hurled out what little food her stomach had.

Her mother lifted the bucket from under the bed and held it up. Tanyaradzwa wiped her mouth with the back of her hand. Her body still shook from the trauma.

Her mother handed her a bottle of mouthwash. "Maybe you shouldn't go back to boarding school, so that I can take care of you. You could go to one of the schools in the neighborhood. I've already talked to your father. He is coming back early from his trip."

"Mama, I'm going to be all right," Tanyaradzwa reassured her.

Her mother sighed, knowing her daughter's stubbornness. "I'll talk to your father then. I'll leave you to rest now . . . Try to eat a few mouthfuls before you sleep, so that you can take your medication."

Tanyaradzwa nodded. She watched as her mother walked toward the door.

"Mama . . ."

She turned.

"I don't hear the rain."

Her mother glanced outside. "The clouds are dispersing."

It was then that Tanyaradzwa knew for certain that the hope she felt could only be sustained by God.

18

Shamiso sat on the veranda next to her grandmother. Two strangers with no conversation. She couldn't stop staring at the old woman's face. It was covered in lines, each one telling a tale of a long and full life. There were dark circles around her eyes and a slight resemblance to her father in the way her lips would twitch.

She could see a handful of boys paving her father's grave with cement. Traces of pain twisted in her gut. She brought her head down and stared at her toes, her throat tight with anger. She would have liked to give a speech or read a poem to say goodbye. But she could barely breathe, let alone speak.

She could hear her father's cousins in the house discussing how his belongings were to be distributed. Custom dictated that the deceased's possessions had to be shared among his loved ones, little souvenirs that would keep his memory close. Shamiso's mother had allowed them to share the few things in those bags. He hadn't owned much, but the little that was in his name had been left to his wife and daughter in a will. It seemed only appropriate that his cousins got whatever few bits were in the bags.

Shamiso watched her mother speak to one of the men who had come to the funeral. He held his hat to his chest and kept his chin slightly down. Shamiso's mother nodded. The two shook hands and Shamiso's mother moved away and sat beside her.

She heard her grandmother offering her mother a place to stay if things got too hard. Shamiso frowned. She knew it had everything to do with their failure to return to the UK; that her father had been the sole provider; that they had little money to their name and, now that her father was gone, they lacked the necessary immigration papers.

She watched her aunt commandeer her cousins, complaining that they were ignorant of their people's culture. Shamiso had no idea what that meant. She saw one of the girls sulk her way to the kitchen. It must have had something to do with the fire that she had been instructed to light. Shamiso wondered whether the girl had even been taught to light it. It was strange how she was expected to have the skill. At the other end of the yard children were scurrying around, completely oblivious to what was going on or why they were here.

The trees in the distance whispered to her. The sky painted the frame of the mountains in dim yellow and thick red. She could see a lot from here. Her grandmother's farm lay on top of a plateau, surrounded by a host of banana trees and overlooking the valley where the fields were. The land had been allocated to her during the land reform program back in 2005. The valley beamed with life, generous in color and soaking up the water that flowed from a ravine close by. It was remarkable how, in this dry weather, little corners of heaven still hid in the country.

Her father had told her how the colonialists had chosen the good land and left the arid parts to the rest of the population. She understood why they must have loved it, but they had asked no one, compensated no one and just taken it as though it belonged to them.

Her father had bitterly opposed his parents' receipt of this beautiful priceless piece of land though. She had never heard him explain it, but from his many articles she suspected it had something to do with how the redistribution had been carried out. Rumor had it the farm had been seized from the previous owner. The men who seized the farm had also asked no one, compensated no one, but took it as though it belonged to them.

Suddenly there was a loud wail. One of the children had fallen and grazed her knee. She watched as one of her uncles ran to the little girl, picked her up and comforted her. There was something about him that reminded her of her father. She wondered if he had ever held her like that and chased away her tears.

She did not remember much of when she was younger. There were moments that time seemed to hold out of reach that she wished she could relive. Then there were future moments that haunted her, the laughs they had never had, the road trips they never took, the stories he had not yet shared with her. The thought of it made her stomach turn. There was so much that still needed to be said and done that she wanted him present for.

She could visualize him in that coffin, the silk of the lining brushing his black suit. His body had looked nothing like him though; his scarred and punctured face haunted her; the broken skin, the swollen lips, the missing ear, the sunken eyes. She basked in the horror of it and found herself hoping the impact of that gruesome car wreck had snatched his life immediately before he felt any pain.

"Shamiso, here's your food." Her grumbling cousin saved her from her thoughts, declaring her presence with an over-powering smell of smoke. It seemed her efforts with the fire had eventually paid off. Shamiso attempted a smile as she received the plate and placed it on her lap. She stared down at the enormous oversized sadza sitting on her plate, waiting to be eaten.

One of her uncles came out of the house holding her father's satchel and sat next to her mother.

"Maiguru," she heard him say, "we are about to start dis-tributing the clothes. Some of his other things will go with you to Harare. We thought maybe since Shamiso will be going to school, she should have her father's satchel."

Her mother said nothing. She stared at the satchel for a while, nodded slightly and passed it to her daughter. All the while Shamiso watched her. It was unlikely that her mother realized it, but she was softly rocking herself again.

The crowd had grown slightly smaller. Some of the peo-ple had left straight after the burial. The remaining guests laughed and chatted and ate and drank and laughed some more. Somehow, the sight of life going forward bothered Shamiso. Death was such a dreary reality. Sooner or later people move on and forget. Only a tiny amount of time had passed, yet it seemed the world was continuing, turning on its axis, done with the life of her father. The lavish theatrics that had been displayed earlier had now fizzled.

"I heard some of the men from the city saying his death was not just an accident. Do you know anything?" her grandmother piped up.

Shamiso's mother raised her head.

Her grandmother continued. "I told him to stop fighting with men hidden in the shadows. What did he want? For his own people not to be in possession of our land?" Shamiso could hear her voice beginning to tremble. "Must I also be ashamed of this very land then? This land that his own father fought for! Were we to starve? Were we to deliberate over the very land that was stolen from us?

"Now look! Shamiso must grow up without a father because of his educated philosophies. Well, here's *my* educated philosophy: we needed this land! You come here with your human rights, but you forget that we tried to have this done properly. But of course the white farmers wouldn't cooperate! Now you are busy pointing fingers, but this was done for you!"

"He was fighting for justice—" Shamiso's mother interrupted.

"Justice? Whose justice? They kept us in pens like animals while they took all the good land and made laws that kept us from buying any of it back! Now you tell me about justice! Why does justice appear when it comes to them? Justice is what my husband did, fighting so that we could get this land!"

Shamiso glanced at her mother, who was staring into the distance with worry painted on her forehead. "The land reform was not done well, Amai. It's not just the white farmers that were punished. There were black farmers who lost their farms! Plus the economy . . ." Shamiso watched her mother trail off at the sharp, piercing look from her grandmother. "Baba-Shamiso only wanted things to be made right," she finished softly, her face tilted downward.

Shamiso's grandmother clicked her tongue in disagreement.

There was silence after that.

19

Three days after the burial, one of Shamiso's uncles managed to organize a job for her mother. It didn't pay much, so she would have to take on other work, but it came with the little cottage they now called home, or at least tried to. Her mother had had a limited education, and the best work she could do was with her hands. So, in exchange for cleaning and taking care of the landlord's house, she would get a roof over their heads and a few dollars in her pocket.

The house belonged to an old couple whose three farms close to the city had been seized during Hondo Yeminda. They had temporarily relocated to Zambia where they bought some land and could resume their business of farming. But they were adamant about not leaving the country for good; after all, it was their home.

The cottage was small; unbearably small, to be precise. It had only been used to house the landlord's maid in the past. Hardly ideal for two people. There was a bathroom and toilet, a room that was both lounge and kitchen, and one bedroom.

Sharing a bed with her mother completely unnerved Shamiso. She had never done that before.

They didn't have much in this new cottage: a creaking three-quarter-sized bed, a broken mirror standing in the corner and a wardrobe for their clothes. In the kitchen was a gel stove on top of a box that served as storage for their pots and cutlery, as well as a small black radio on the floor and two plastic chairs. Her father's boxes took up the remaining space.

Their apartment back in Slough had been quite comfy, but now there was hardly enough money to make ends meet as it was, let alone allow them to ship their belongings here. Shamiso despised the whole situation, but there was nothing to be done. Her father had been the sole breadwinner, and till his life insurance policy paid out, she and her mother were powerless and broke.

She stood by the window in the living room, or was it a kitchen? She could see her mother's silhouette in the kitchen window of the main house. She seemed to be scrubbing something, the sink perhaps. After all, there were no dirty dishes since no one was home.

Shamiso headed for the radio. Perhaps a little music would lift her spirits. As she fumbled with the tuner, wondering why the radio was unresponsive, her eye picked up the notice that had been in the mailbox earlier. Of course, load-shedding!

The silence was too much. Frustration bit at her. This was the place that her father had loved, but it was impossible for her to love it in the same way. She felt as though she was trapped in a nightmare she couldn't leave, as though someone had pulled the rug from beneath her and stolen her life in the process.

20

Horror loomed in the hallway and clung to the walls of the hospital. The place reeked of medicine, pain and disease. The intensity of the atmosphere made Tanyaradzwa uneasy. She sat on the chair, her foot nervously tapping on the floor. There was not a lot to distract her. Once in a while some uniformed person would walk past, but that was it.

Tanyaradzwa saw her mother's lips move as she spoke to one of the nurses at the reception. She nodded a lot as the nurse spoke. Tanyaradzwa sighed. The hospital was not accepting individual health insurance anymore. It had become a financial risk. Right beside them, another nurse was speaking to a bald old man who seemed well acquainted with fatigue. Tanyaradzwa could hear the nurse explaining that the old man would need to pay for his treatment in cash. At least they had known about this; her oncologist had warned them in advance. She watched the old man walk out of the hospital.

Tanyaradzwa blinked slowly. Cancer was exhausting everyone.

As her eyes followed the old man, she caught a glimpse of her father pacing up and down just outside the hospital entrance, one hand holding his phone to his ear and the other swimming around in the air. He had been at it for the past twenty minutes or so. There had been a lot of brow-brushing and head-scratching. He needed a large sum of money from the bank, not only for bills relating to her treatment, but for his business as well. It had been announced just that morning that citizens would only be allowed to withdraw a maximum of a few thousand Zim dollars. This had created panic. She looked at his folded face, brushed with lines of stress. He was trying to get money: money he knew he had in the bank.

"Tanyaradzwa Pfumojena! Tanyaradzwa Pfumojena."

She turned and looked at her mother, who nodded, then signaled at her father. He pointed to the phone and continued pacing. Tanyaradzwa followed the nurse down the hallway. The farther they went, the more vile the medicinal taste became.

The nurse indicated for her to sit down. "Tanyaradzwa Pfumojena," she said, reading from her clipboard.

She smiled, which only made Tanyaradzwa more uneasy. She watched as the nurse drew a long syringe from the tray. The noise of the plastic ripping was elaborate. Her heart sped up. She had been through all this before, but it was something she would never get used to.

Her eyes stayed fixed on the nurse's arm as she connected the little plastic portal of the drip bag to the end of the syringe. Tanyaradzwa swallowed again. The nurse's cold, gloved hand rubbed her arm and tapped it for a vein.

"Breathe . . ." she instructed and smiled that alarming smile. "You've done this before, no?"

Tanyaradzwa nodded.

"Don't worry, it'll only take a minute." The nurse rubbed some sterilizing ointment on her arm.

Tanyaradzwa held her breath, eyes on the syringe and heart thudding rapidly.

She flinched at the bite of the needle.

PART THREE
Six weeks after that

21

Life had begun to settle into a new kind of rhythm. Tinotenda sat on the teacher's table in front of the class like he always did, reading the paper. Like any other Tuesday, the students half listened as he read aloud, their faces dark and closed off. But unlike any other Tuesday, Mr. Mpofu wasn't present. He had not delivered the paper. So there was no speech about keeping them updated on the goings-on of the country. Today, because of the strike, not a single teacher had showed up, although Tinotenda claimed to have seen a bunch of them in the staffroom, probably only there to ensure that the students were not completely abandoned.

Shamiso wondered about Mr. Mpofu. Murmurings floated around that a fight had broken out at the local bar close to the school, where most of the teachers retired for a drink after work. The story was that Mr. Mpofu's political views had instigated a brawl and he had been crushed like a wild berry underfoot. Shamiso had no idea if the rumors were true.

She stared at the oak tree outside. She could hear Tinotenda reading on. Election results had now been released, nearly a month late. The paper announced a possible rerun of the election, which had unleashed chaos. People everywhere, even in the class, were on edge, exchanging different views.

Shamiso glanced at her wristwatch, wondering if Mr. Mpofu would still show. He was never late, regardless of the strike. In fact, he was one of the few teachers that made it to class at all. She had heard the others joking about a time he had had the flu and had wheezed and coughed his way through the whole lesson; not that the students had remotely appreciated that.

She peeked at her watch again, realizing the seconds were crawling by. Tinotenda was now narrating a made-up version of what had happened at the bar. From the way he told the story, it sounded like he had been there, having sneaked out of the hostels at night. Shamiso rolled her eyes. He did not exactly own up to it, but his story had too many inconsistencies. She guessed he had been at the scene on other occasions and was now trying to imagine what had happened that day.

Tanyaradzwa seemed to be the only other person in the class whose mind was drifting elsewhere.

Shamiso bent her head into her book. She could feel the weight of Tanyaradzwa's eyes on her, but she scribbled some answers as though she hadn't noticed.

Tanyaradzwa shook her head and turned toward the front again.

She fanned her shirt, opened her top button and loosened her tie. The heat was overwhelming. It was strange how everyone else seemed to be coping with it. She lowered her head onto the desk and, as she did so, a pool of saliva collected in her mouth. She swallowed faster in a bid to keep up. Before she could register what was going on, her morning porridge had made it to the floor, and her mouth tasted vile and bitter. Not much stayed with her after that.

Shamiso's reflexes kicked in and she pushed her chair back and made her way to where Tanyaradzwa was lying on the floor.

A little crowd circled around her, but most of the class stayed at their desks, staring.

Shamiso called out to Tanyaradzwa, but it seemed the girl's body had given up. Without thinking, she gasped to Paida and two other girls to help lift Tanyaradzwa and started leading the way to the school clinic.

As they went out the door, Shamiso glanced back at the class.

They were whispering among themselves, faces lit up with disgust.

22

Shamiso found herself in the middle of whatever was happening to Tanyaradzwa. She sat on a wooden bench outside the school clinic, wondering how she had gotten to this place. In that brief moment back in the classroom, a kindness, like insanity, had gripped her and she had sprung into action. Now she had been sentenced to the clinic bench for the whole afternoon. Paida and her two friends stood a small distance away.

The school van had not been fueled, of course, because of the scarcity of petrol. And because Tanyaradzwa seemed to be coming around, the school nurse had asked the girls if they would accompany her to the hostel on foot.

Shamiso felt trapped. She could hear Paida tell the other girls how her father had treated the family to a holiday in Zanzibar for her brother's eighteenth birthday, accompanied by the gift of a whole farm afterward.

"I mean, what will he do with a whole farm? My brother wasn't so pleased with it. He just wanted the latest Xbox."

Shamiso scratched her neck. An afternoon with Paida was the price she had to pay for compassion.

Paida and her friends indulged in giggles and whispers, evidently enjoying their excuse not to be in class. Shamiso turned to see if there was any movement from the nurse's office.

Shamiso approached the other girls. "Do you know how long this is going to take?"

They stopped and looked at her.

"Dude, you smell of smoke." Paida laughed as she drew away.

Shamiso stepped back as her heart began to pound. The other girls wrinkled their noses and continued their conversation.

She strolled slowly to the newspaper stand by the door before surreptitiously sniffing at her cardigan. She knew where the smoke had come from. She rubbed the itch creeping up her right arm.

The girls' chatter pricked at her as she reached the stand. Then cold paralysis struck. She stared in horror at the paper on the metal rack. She reached out for it, both hands shivering. Her father's picture filled half the page. Her heart froze, stuck mid-beat. Holding her breath, she unfolded the paper and read the bottom half. The lump in her throat tightened.

"Maybe Tanyaradzwa's pregnant," she heard Paida say, and all three erupted into gasps and giggles.

"It's always the quiet ones that do such things, honestly," one of the girls agreed.

Shamiso struggled to breathe. Her ears were saturated with the noise and laughter that escaped Paida's mouth. The same sound that had escaped the girl's lips the day she spread those lies about her father. The lies that kept being spread around and around and around. They were everywhere!

"She has been sick a lot actually," Paida went on, drawing closer to her friends.

Shamiso shut her eyes. Reality spiraled out of her grasp, gaining momentum and sucking her into its vortex. She had nothing to hold on to. The pressure of it all fizzed within her. She needed everything to stop: the noise, the laughter, the lies.

"Shut up!" she hissed from the stand. The three girls stared at her in amazement. Her breath gained pace, galloping to relieve her thirsty lungs.

Paida raised one eyebrow, folded her arms and took a step back. "We weren't talking to you."

Shamiso stared at her, heart still pounding. Anger took hold of her, pushing her body toward Paida and raising her hand.

A sharp pain cut through her palm and she heard a piercing shriek from Paida. Her hands trembled and her mind whirled. All those things the paper had said about her father! She knew they weren't true. Her father had never held a single pint in his life. He couldn't have caused his own death!

23

Tanyaradzwa liked to think of her body as a mysterious bag of codes and tunes that had to be kept in balance. She knew that if ignored it could spike into tantrums that would cause a perfect disaster.

She swirled the gulp of water she had taken. It had been in her mouth long enough to warm up. She looked at the capsules in her hand, wishing they would just go away, then tilted her head back and dropped them into her open mouth. Her throat held them there, their bitter sting slipping downward. Little aches nudged at her back. She had been lying here for too long.

A soft breeze whistled through the window. Tanyaradzwa pulled herself up and out of her bed. The fresh air was so tempting. She stepped outside and felt the breeze dance around her, cooling her feverish body. She made her way to the laundry room, a short distance from her hostel. The light still shone through the open door.

She could hear a little trickle pouring from the tap into one of the washing basins. The council had cut off the water again earlier. Someone must have forgotten to close the tap after checking if the water was back on. She walked into the laundry room to turn it off and, as she did so, spotted someone sitting on the stairs leading out of the room.

She stopped.

"Shamiso?"

Shamiso turned to face Tanyaradzwa. Her hand moved out of sight.

"What are you doing out here?" Tanyaradzwa asked in surprise.

Shamiso turned her back to Tanyaradzwa and pulled the sleeves of her pajamas over her palms.

"What does it look like?" She brought the cigarette to her mouth. Tanyaradzwa stared for a second, then sat down beside her. Shamiso searched Tanyaradzwa's face for judgment. It wasn't there.

"What are you doing here?" Shamiso asked.

"Air," Tanyaradzwa replied.

They sat there for a moment, uncertainty hovering between them.

"I heard you slapped Paida?"

Shamiso looked away. A small smile escaped her lips. "More like my palm slipped onto her face."

The girls laughed awkwardly, stretching the silence while each tried to work out how the conversation might continue.

"If you did it for me, you should be careful. It's actually starting to look like you might be growing a heart there," Tanyaradzwa advised in her soft voice.

Shamiso smiled.

Silence settled once more.

"I'm not pregnant."

"I know."

Tanyaradzwa hesitated. "It's . . . cancer."

Shamiso kept her gaze firmly in the distance and pulled in another drag of smoke as if she hadn't heard. The silence stayed with them for a minute longer. Tanyaradzwa's eyes rested on Shamiso, waiting for the pity that usually came. Shamiso turned to her. Her eyes were quiet. They offered an incredible relief. In that moment, Tanyaradzwa did not feel like the girl with a deadly disease.

"Are you going to die?"

Tanyaradzwa kept her gaze on Shamiso. Her right hand reached for her neck and pressed lightly against the little mass inside her. She did not know how to feel about the question.

"Well, aren't we all?" she replied.

Shamiso looked at her and smiled.

"You probably need this more than me then?" She extended the lit cigarette to Tanyaradzwa.

Tanyaradzwa burst into peals of laughter. Her laugh lingered, ringing out for longer than it was supposed to; almost as if there was a broken car nearby whose keys had jammed and now simply refused to restart.

24

Students moved more quietly, sticking to their little groups as they headed back to the classrooms for evening prep after another long day. The teachers stood their ground and continued with the strike. Shamiso walked alone, wondering what purpose school served while the teachers were still on strike. But the principal had made it clear that students were expected to go about "business as usual."

It didn't feel much like business as usual. On a normal day, the students would already have been seated, waiting for the second siren to sound. Yet, Paida and her friends chattered away behind her, relaxed in spite of the time, and the girls in front of her were having a heated conversation, the volume rising as they explained things to each other in competing voices.

Shamiso continued along the jacaranda avenue to the classrooms and felt a slight tap on her shoulder. She turned to see Tanyaradzwa walking beside her, holding her books to her chest.

"Hey!" Tanyaradzwa called.

Shamiso frowned. "Your voice . . . ?"

"I think I'm getting a cold, that's all," Tanyaradzwa explained, before coughing into her elbow.

Shamiso shuffled in silence alongside her, unsure of what to say.

"You want some?" Tanyaradzwa asked eventually.

Shamiso looked at the pack of maputi in Tanyaradzwa's hand and smiled. She had hated the salty taste of it at first, but it had grown on her. She reached her hand into the back of her satchel, produced a packet of her own and waved it playfully in Tanyaradzwa's face. The girls burst into cackles of laughter, leaving Tanyaradzwa coughing.

In her merriment, Shamiso didn't realize that the yellow envelope, the one with her father's writing on it, had been pulled out in the process. It dangled on the bridge of the satchel's pocket, contemplating freefall.

The siren sounded noisily, heralding the start of prep; everyone ought to have already been seated by now. The students around them started running.

"Go on, run," Tanyaradzwa advised in her voice of broken whispers. The two girls could see Mr. Mpofu walking toward them, one hand in his pocket and the other carrying a small travel bag. He had a slight limp, and his lip had a bruise as if he had been fighting. The girls looked at each other, Tanyaradzwa more nervously than Shamiso.

"Pfumojena . . . Muloy . . ." he called as he got closer, his free hand now softly stroking his beard as though it were a pampered royal cat.

Shamiso stepped up her pace. Tanyaradzwa tried to increase hers. Paida and her friends ran behind them. The yellow envelope fell.

"Did you . . . happen to . . . hear the siren?" he asked, now standing by the main gate.

Shamiso rolled her eyes. While her attention was on the teacher, Paida snatched up the envelope and hid it among her books, excitement hopping through her veins at the thought of having something that belonged to Shamiso.

"Sir, I am not feeling well so I was unable to . . ." Tanyaradzwa began to explain. Mr. Mpofu raised his hand in the air, halting her monologue. All the while, his eyes were on Shamiso.

"Muloy . . . are you . . . unwell too?"

Shamiso shook her head.

He glanced behind her.

"Paida, shouldn't you know better?"

Paida remained silent.

"Then I believe detention tomorrow might help your hearing next time the siren sounds." The girls began to plead but stopped, reading the stern look on his face. He moved out of the way, allowing them to continue to prep. They carried on, scared to look back in case they turned to salt.

25

Paida dumped her backpack in her room after class and stared at the yellow envelope that Shamiso had dropped. Curiosity hit her over the head and she wondered what the envelope contained. Knowing that what she was about to do was wrong, she checked to see if anyone was behind her, before opening the flap of the envelope and pulling out the folded sheets of paper. Her eyes scurried over the first page. She could hear voices in Shamiso's room, her roommates laughing at something.

At first a smug smile came over her as she realized who Shamiso's father was. His name signed in block letters at the bottom of the final page.

She turned over to the next page. Her heart began to race with adrenaline. He seemed to be chasing a story.

Then fear gripped her by the throat.

26

Nights rolled over, and time did its work, breeding a friendship between Shamiso and Tanyaradzwa. Their storms roared, but there was a strange sort of peace to be found in distraction.

Shamiso still struggled occasionally. In the back of her mind lay a warning that if she allowed this friendship to attach to her, it would tear her up when the clock stopped and the velcro had to be unstuck.

But as they sat on those same stairs by the exit of the laundry room, she threw caution aside and plunged in. The sky was a sea of stars and she could hear Tanyaradzwa wheezing quietly over the hum of crickets.

"He—my dad . . . he died in a car crash," Shamiso whispered, the words hiding in the coarseness of her voice. "He hit a tree, in the middle of nowhere, no traffic."

She swallowed.

The lump.

"You know—" she pressed through the pain—"he left us to come here because he said he had a lead on a big story. He . . ." She choked.

Tanyaradzwa propped herself up and watched her friend struggling to contain the flow of tears.

Shamiso forced a brittle smile. "I wish I knew what really happened to him. You don't just ram into a tree, right?" She pulled her little cigarette box from her pocket. "You don't mind, do you?" she asked, drawing out a smoke.

Tanyaradzwa shook her head.

Shamiso lifted it to her lips and held it there.

"The papers claim he caused the accident, but he never drank in his life." She looked at Tanyaradzwa, her face in a knot. "Tell me, how am I meant to love a murder scene?"

Tanyaradzwa looked confused.

"This place—it's the reason why he's gone . . . yet it's the only thing that ties me to him. How am I supposed to love it?"

Tanyaradzwa recognized the pain. It looked different on Shamiso, but she knew it all the same. She could see defeat wrapping its icy fingers around her friend. It was a slippery slope. Her eyes welled up in sympathy.

Shamiso wiped her nose with the back of her hand.

Tanyaradzwa hesitated, knowing fully well that comforting an injured soul was a mammoth task. But then it struck her: healing is what they had in common. She took a gulp of air and closed her eyes as she imagined it gently touching the broken pieces inside her.

"Your dad, the journalist . . . ?" she confirmed.

Shamiso nodded.

"He wrote hope into people," Tanyaradzwa offered. "I think your father loved this place for a reason. Give it time, and once the pain isn't all you feel, you will start to see it too. No, things are not the way they should be. They will not go back to how they were before, but it will be better than it is now. The pain will go away."

Shamiso's face twisted into a scowl. She sniffed. "How can you possibly know that?"

Tanyaradzwa smiled. "Well, hope is our only wing out of a stormy gale, isn't it?"

Shamiso sat there for a moment, frozen. The words circled around her, and she could almost hear her father's voice. She knew the quote well; she'd heard it once too often.

His last affair with ink and paper had been a heartfelt oration of the olden days robbed from his beautiful country; of the many children of the soil pushed out of the country by the creeping cancer; of how he had been unable to fly back home from the diaspora to bury his father because the airfare could do more important things like paying for the burial. His grand exit—an articulate, impassioned piece that Shamiso had read so many times she almost knew all the words—was the last memory she had of her father. She turned back to Tanyaradzwa.

"Let me guess—you're one of those the-glass-is-always-half-full kind of people, aren't you?"

Tanyaradzwa smiled and looked at the night sky. Shamiso could see her silhouette moving in the moonlight. Flashbacks of her father trapped her, pressing against her brain. She could almost see him, spinning around in his swivel chair with his pen in his mouth, trying to write. She could practically smell the cold coffee in the mug on his desk.

"If you hung out with me more, you'd know how very untrue that statement is. I'm definitely one of those people who thinks that if the glass is half empty, you might as well drink whatever is in it," Tanyaradzwa replied at last, looking

Shamiso in the eye. Moonlight danced across her left cheek. "But I know your dad was right about hope."

Shamiso narrowed her eyes. She wouldn't listen to such talk. "If you ask me, hope is a dangerous thing. It can be a leap into endless darkness."

Shamiso's heart pumped as she walked briskly back to the hostel. It was clear from the pace of her feet that she was running from something.

27

The students went about their business, hoping that their history teacher would keep striking and not come to class. There had been talk that the school's parents' committee was arranging for incentives to be given to the teachers to compensate for their outrageously low salaries. The students, led by Tinotenda, debated whether or not this was a good idea.

Shamiso and Tanyaradzwa sat in their usual seats; Tanyaradzwa was pretending everything was all right between them, while Shamiso kept her nose buried in her book. Suddenly, she grabbed her satchel and searched for her schedule. She peered inside the bag. The envelope was gone! She flung open her desk and checked to see if she had put it in there.

"Have you seen my yellow envelope?" she asked Tanyaradzwa, her face set to show that it was not a call for a truce. Tanyaradzwa shook her head. Shamiso cursed herself for not opening it sooner. She wondered if she had dropped it or if someone had taken it. She put the satchel down, trying to comfort herself with the fact that she still had parts of her father in the articles he had published.

Mr. Mpofu appeared at the door. The class fell silent. He held a rolled newspaper in his hand and seemed to have fresh bruises on his face. Tinotenda immediately stood up, heading toward him to get the paper. The teacher waved him down.

"Muloy," he said.

Shamiso's eyes left her book. She heaved in frustration as she anticipated another squabble. Mr. Mpofu signaled her over with the paper in his hand.

"I don't read," she protested.

"But can you?" he asked, walking slowly into the room, his other hand still in his pocket.

"Yes." She smiled at the absurdity of the question.

"Well . . . it's settled then," he said, extending the paper in her direction.

She stood up and headed to the front of the room, facing Paida who sat there as always. Paida sat quietly, avoiding any eye contact with Shamiso. She moved her backpack to her lap. Shamiso breathed in, trying to make her annoyance dissolve.

Mr. Mpofu handed her the paper. Shamiso unrolled it and looked at the front page.

"This is an old paper," she said in surprise.

"I know . . . We already celebrated Independence Day last month, but since your history teacher . . . is not coming in today . . ." He paused as though he had forgotten that he was in the middle of a sentence. "I thought you could read one of the best pieces ever written commemorating our independence. No matter what happens . . . you kids must know we have a beautiful country, with a beautiful spirit. Don't forget to fight for it when you must."

The class listened in confusion. It sounded like a farewell speech of sorts.

Shamiso sighed. She slowly read the headline, emphasizing her disapproval of this whole exercise. Her eyes slid to the tiny print with the journalist's name. Her lips beat her mind to it and read out the name first. Her hands clenched the paper. Paida pulled her backpack closer to her. Tanyaradzwa perked up.

Shamiso turned to Mr. Mpofu. He smiled softly and nodded.

She blinked away the tears as she watched him walk out of the room. She sat down on the teacher's table, voices in her head screaming at her to run. She cleared her throat and pushed herself to read out the short excerpt from her father's archives.

28

The trouble with swallowing your pride is that, like any other thick bone, it can get stuck in your throat. And like any reasonable person, the only remedy Shamiso knew was to drink a lot of water. She sat restlessly, trying to avoid looking at Tanyaradzwa. She refilled her glass and took a gulp. Last night had been intense.

The girls sat in the dining hall among a sea of chattering students. They waited for the servers to bring the food to their tables. The hall echoed with clunking spoons and cups, students eager for their morning tea. It seemed to be taking a little longer than usual. Finally, the uniformed servers exited the kitchen to the sound of cheering as they pushed trolleys heavy with food bowls, placing one at each table. Once they had done so, silence fell as the prayer was recited by one of the students. The silence was broken by a resounding amen.

As the bowls were uncovered, they unleashed a thick aroma of fat cakes together with shock and protests.

A prefect stood at the front of the dining hall. "Students, due to the situation in the country, we have been unable to acquire bread for your teatime. But you'll be pleased to see an alternative has been provided. Please note that the school is doing everything it can to ensure that you are well taken care of. Your understanding and cooperation are greatly appreciated . . ."

The students were not impressed, but most of them accepted the change. Tanyaradzwa sat watching the girl at the top of the table pour tea from the giant teapot into the ten mugs, one for each person. It was the first time the tea had been black, but the reason for that was the same as the story behind the fat cakes.

A prefect signaled for Tanyaradzwa. Shamiso watched as she followed him. As she went outside, Tanyaradzwa saw her father's car parked under the proud jacaranda trees. Her heart thudded with excitement. He was standing close by, talking to the principal.

A short distance away Paida also stood by a red Mercedes, balancing two huge boxes and talking to a uniformed man, probably a driver. This had happened every week since the food shortages. The two of them seemed to be the only ones allowed regular visitors. It made sense for Tanyaradzwa because she was ill. For Paida, however, it must have been thanks to her father's big name. She would get two boxes of food every week and was never shy to share the information though she was not so generous with the food. Everyone else was struggling to get supplies. Paida seemed to be struggling as well, but with a better problem. From the quiver of her shoulders, it looked as if the boxes were too heavy.

As Tanyaradzwa approached her father, she prepared herself for the same talk they had every time. He would insist that she should come home; she would insist that she had to stay.

"You look strong," he said, extending his hand to greet her. She smiled as she tightened her collar.

"We are taking care of her," the principal reassured him.

"Thank you very much for making sure she is well," her father said, his face bright with gratitude.

The principal nodded and excused herself.

"How are you, Baba?" Tanyaradzwa asked, clasping her hands in respect. She knew he did not like being called Dad.

"I hope you are studying hard," he said as he opened the door of the car for her to get in. Tanyaradzwa slid into the passenger's seat and waited. She guessed her father wanted to speak in private. He had told her time and again that she should not forget how privileged she was to be getting these regular visits when it was against school policy. And that flaunting it would be an insult to the other students.

"Most of the teachers are still on strike," she informed him.

He nodded. "You must not let that slow your pace though. We'll arrange for a tutor during the holidays."

She waited for him to ask her again to come home with him. But for once he talked about everything else instead.

"For now you must keep studying on your own. I brought you these textbooks," he said, handing her a pile of glossy new books. She smiled and put them on her lap. They sat there in silence.

"Well, I can't stay for long or I will miss my flight. I brought your medicine and a few eats," he said at last, handing her a plastic bag full of food. The brands were all foreign.

"There's no Mazoe in the stores, so you'll have to make do with that juice," he said, patting her on the back.

Tanyaradzwa smiled at him. She knew he was going to Botswana again. The recent announcement that all businesses were to be majority-owned by citizens had scared off his investors. He was trying to move the business out of the country.

Her father said goodbye and set off. She watched his Range Rover drive away, leaving a trail of dust in the air.

Shamiso walked out of the dining hall with the rest of the students and made her way toward Tanyaradzwa. She watched her for a while, noticing for the first time that her friend's body looked scrawny, fragile. She was losing weight.

"Everything all right?" Shamiso asked, using curiosity and concern to wash down her pride.

Tanyaradzwa broke into a mighty grin. "We have food," she said. "That's all right, isn't it?"

She opened her bag of goodies, a peace offering that inspired both of them to laugh at the same time.

29

There are three main things to remember on a blazing hot day: drink lots of water, stay in the shade as much as possible and don't get caught with a stolen chicken's scrawny legs dangling from your jersey. The heat is brutal, but an enraged principal is much worse.

Shamiso stood beside Tanyaradzwa at the head of the assembly lines outside by the school quad. They could see the crowd of students turning to the left and cracking up. The laughter spread like a virus. The girls lifted themselves on their tiptoes, trying to see what was causing it. The gazes of the students moved slowly from the left to the front. Shamiso's gaze followed Tinotenda as he was hurled onto the stage by the principal, his right arm in her firm grip. His face showed a unique mix of fear and mischief. The school tried to suppress giggles that were no doubt inspired by the terrified white broiler chicken under Tinotenda's cardigan. The boy seemed to be under strict orders to make sure it did not run free.

The principal stood facing the students, her face stern and her spectacles balancing on the bridge of her nose.

"Good morning, school," her sharp voice rang out, sending the students into immediate silence. "As you all know, most of our teachers are on strike. The school administration is doing everything it can to ensure that the situation is resolved. As I told you last week, the instruction from the Ministry of Education is that students remain in school . . ."

The principal went on, talking about the strike and the dietary changes. Shamiso watched Tinotenda, who still stood by the principal's side. His once clucking chicken was now calm and seemed to be enjoying the attention. The principal's speech continued for several minutes. Her voice grew quiet, her eyes roaming over the room. The students dared not even sneeze.

"Here at Oakwood, we do not tolerate stealing! Even with the drastic change of diet in your dining hall. I've called you all here because Tinotenda has decided to bond with one of the school farm's chickens, as you can see." This last part sent the students into a roar of laughter.

She remained serious; not a single facial muscle flinched. "Under normal circumstances, Tinotenda would be suspended. But because of his vital role in preparing for the school band's participation at the national music festival, alternative discipline will be administered." She pushed her spectacles up again. "For now, the school supports this new friendship he has made with one of our very own . . ."

Laughter.

Shamiso's eyes bulged as Tinotenda's wry smile disappeared. He fidgeted, avoiding the crowd. She glanced at Tanyaradzwa, whose muffled laugh rippled from under her cupped hands. Shamiso smiled; her expression a fusion of nerves and amusement at the sight of the chicken cozying up to the boy's chest.

"I am very disappointed in you, Tinotenda! You are here for the sole purpose of learning, not socializing with school animals." She paused to allow more laughter. "Students, I want to make it very clear that nothing has changed. You are still expected to focus on your studies. Anyone caught on the wrong side of the rules will be dealt with accordingly. Do I make myself clear?"

She turned to the boy who was now looking down in embarrassment. Humiliation was certainly a dish best served in public.

30

The sun sank into the horizon as the moon stared it down. The sight always brimmed with magic. Students were already walking back to their hostels, before heading on for supper. Study time would follow soon after.

Shamiso walked to the music room, wondering why Tanyaradzwa had insisted she come to the rehearsal. As she drew near, she could hear the band playing in the music room. A team of four students; three boys and Tanyaradzwa who met every week to rehearse. The walls in the room were different from those in the other classes. The band was set up on one side and, on the other, different instruments sat by the shelves. They were practicing for the annual music festival whose likelihood of taking place, given the situation in the country, stood uncertain.

She opened the door softly and made her way inside. All heads turned toward her as the sole of her shoe tapped on the wooden floor.

Tanyaradzwa immediately stopped playing and made her way to Shamiso. "We've just gotten the harmonies nailed. I can't wait for you to hear this," she said.

Shamiso smiled.

"Can we finish with this first and you ladies can gossip afterward?" Tinotenda bellowed.

Tanyaradzwa rubbed Shamiso's arm. "As soon as we're done, okay?"

Shamiso nodded. She watched Tanyaradzwa return to her seat. Tinotenda stood close to the white walls at the back of the room, fastening the little wooden mouthpiece to his saxophone. Shamiso wondered how well he could play. All he ever seemed to do was clown around. Another boy fumbled with his guitar, possibly tuning it, and the third lurked over his bongo drums. Tanyaradzwa sat in the middle, mbira on her lap.

Tinotenda signaled for the music to start and the instruments sang.

Shamiso watched as Tanyaradzwa strummed away at the mbira. She had a way with the instrument. There was something about the sparkle in her eye that reminded Shamiso of her father. Her stomach tightened.

She had never heard such a beautiful collision of instruments. The melody tied everything into a weeping wind. The saxophone synchronized with the dancing strums of the mbira. The sweet rings of the guitar strings pulled that melody and thrust it against the confident beats of the bongo drums.

Tanyaradzwa's rusty voice pulled the chords together, riding with the harmony of the song. Shamiso marveled at the level of talent. The music messed with her memories and raised buried ghosts. In a bid to shut out the sadness, she closed her eyes and concentrated on the notes of the music. As she listened, the music began to change. Tanyaradzwa continued to sing, but her voice was unraveling into whispers.

Tinotenda stopped playing and stared. Tanyaradzwa pulled through, her fingers strumming the mbira as though nothing was wrong. The other two boys stopped playing too, but she ploughed on with her whispering song.

And then suddenly her left hand let go of the mbira. Shamiso watched as the African guitar tumbled to the floor. Little drops of blood leaked from Tanyaradzwa's nostrils. A deafening din blasted Shamiso's ears. Sound stood still. All she could see were lips moving. Her mouth dried up. She hit a desk from behind. She turned in panic. Her eyes scurried around the room, her breath breaking into desperate gasps. It was that thing again, that thing in her throat. She knew Tanyaradzwa lay there on the floor, but she could not tear her eyes from the abandoned mbira beside her.

Her mind screamed as the three boys hoisted Tanyaradzwa out of the room. She watched Tanyaradzwa's lifeless arms wave in the air. Shamiso could barely move. Sounds, noises, screams shot through her ears. She closed her eyes and fought to breathe.

31

Shamiso lay in her bed back in the hostel, begging sleep to come. Evening prep had been canceled due to another episode of load-shedding. The corridors were almost silent. Just a few rooms glowed with candlelight; a sign of the overly diligent.

Shamiso had been tossing and turning for a while. Her mind taunted her with crawling fears of loss. The fears grew bigger, feeding on her indulgence of them. She turned to face the direction of the door. Tanyaradzwa's bed sat there, bare and empty, mocking her.

She had gathered from the other students that a man in a white Range Rover had come to collect Tanyaradzwa and her belongings. In her cowardice, Shamiso had stayed in the classroom, pretending to study. It had been too much for her to stomach.

She fidgeted again.

The itch crept up on her.

She had not had a night to herself in a while. No one was watching. She reached for the little box under her pillow and headed to the laundry room, conversations with Tanyaradzwa playing over in her mind. The stairs felt like a burden. She remembered the hidden corner she had first visited and hurried there.

Shamiso opened her little box and stared. Only one cigarette was left. She knew once she smoked this, there would be nothing left to numb her. Unable to resist, she drew it out, brought the lighter to its tip and raised the filter to her lips. She could feel the smoke hitting the back of her head and calming her insides.

Just then she heard footsteps. She crawled from the exposure of the light into the shadows.

"How much do you have?" she heard.

"A couple of thousands."

"Nah, tomorrow those won't buy much. I'd rather you do my homework for a week."

Shamiso knew that voice. She peeped out from behind the wall. Paida stood there holding several bags of crisps and talking to another girl from their class! It seemed like some sort of trade.

"Do you smell that?" Paida asked suddenly. "It smells like cigarettes."

Shamiso drew into the cover of the wall dropped the cigarette and held still. The cigarette released a light swirl of smoke. Paida's footsteps headed in her direction, so she reached for the butt with her foot and stamped it out as quietly as possible.

"Paida, I've got to get back before they realize I'm missing," the other voice murmured.

The footsteps halted and changed direction. Shamiso sighed in relief. She dragged herself back to the hostel. The corridors were still pitch-black. As she tiptoed toward her room, a sudden light met her eyes. She could make out the outline of a hand holding a flashlight.

"Where are you coming from?" She heard Paida's voice! Shamiso covered her eyes, lifting her right hand and exposing her sacred secret box.

"What's that?" Paida asked, her voice getting excited.

Shamiso tried to pull it out of sight but it was too late. Paida had already spotted it. The lights beamed back on. The girls blinked as their eyes adjusted.

Shamiso stood there, unsure what to do. "I can explain . . ." she started.

"I dare you," Paida taunted, her left eyebrow raised. "Listen, I can keep my mouth shut—for a price."

Shamiso shook her head.

"What are you girls doing up?" The matron's voice echoed as she walked toward them, her hair wild, as though she had been wrestling a possessed cat.

Paida folded her hands, enjoying the calamity that was about to fall.

PART FOUR
the next day

32

As *Tanyaradzwa staggered to the reception in the doctor's office she could hear the news on the radio. The zeros were being slashed again. It hardly made sense to say bread cost a trillion dollars. It made sense that the reserve bank was doing something about it.*

As she entered the lobby, she noticed the overwhelming absence of human life. Only the receptionist was there, sitting behind a computer, watching something with her earphones plugged in while the radio jabbered on. As she took a seat, Tanyaradzwa quickly adjusted her shirt and sat up straight; she didn't want the receptionist to think she was dying.

She had left her father somewhere in the corridor. He had been on the phone, shouting at someone, again. The inflation had really done a number on him. Midnight seemed to have fallen on most of his investments and they were now turning to pumpkins. Inflation played a cruel bargain with the currency too. The zeros kept changing their minds. Her father had spent all morning trying to buy some US dollars on the black market. He had talked to a guy who knew a guy who worked with a guy who said he could help him out. Her mother had traveled to South Africa for work so Tanyaradzwa had to make do with her distracted father. She didn't blame him really. She understood the stress he was under.

"Tanyaradzwa?" the receptionist called.

Tanyaradzwa smiled. Though she did not have the energy to speak, she stood up with her own version of confidence. She pulled out a wad of cash and handed it to the reception- ist, watching as the lady meticulously counted the money, careful to make sure that it was all there. Once her hand brushed over the last note, she looked at Tanyaradzwa.

"Er, did you come alone?" she asked.

Tanyaradzwa shook her head.

"You see, the consultation fee has gone up," the reception- ist explained, shame leaking from her voice.

Tanyaradzwa looked at her in bewilderment. They had only increased the fees the day before; now they seemed to have done so again.

The receptionist smiled as she heard her father's voice coming from the hallway. "You can go in. I will speak to your father about the fee."

Tanyaradzwa nodded and pulled herself into the doctor's office. She walked slowly but held her head up. The doc- tor sat there, one hand scribbling something and the other holding the phone to her ear. She smiled and signaled to Tan- yaradzwa to sit down. Her lips were colored bright red. Tanyaradzwa had not seen her with much makeup before. She walked toward the chair and carefully lowered herself into it, then waited. The poster on the wall now hung by its ear. The fan still rotated back and forth but this time the gen- erator hummed in the background.

"*I'm sorry about that,*" the doctor said at last as she placed the receiver down. "*How are you feeling?*"

"*A little weak, but I'm fine,*" she managed.

The doctor swung in her chair while she looked at her. "*You actually look quite weak, Tanyaradzwa.*"

Tanyaradzwa fidgeted, detecting the little wave of pity in the doctor's voice. She tried to sit up and keep her back straight.

"*Did you come alone? Where are your parents?*"

"*Baba is on the phone.*"

"*Uh . . .*" the doctor said, before flipping through Tanyaradzwa's file. She scribbled something. The door opened.

"*Mr. Pfumojena, please come in,*" the doctor said.

Tanyaradzwa's father sat down next to his daughter. He wiped his wet brow and pulled the chair closer.

"*I'm sorry about that. You know, with the economy, we're all just trying to make things work,*" he said, attempting to make small talk.

The doctor smiled. "*The cancer seems rather aggressive and I'm worried that we're running out of time. If you had come forward like we . . .*" The doctor bit her tongue and took a deep breath. "*We could keep on at chemo; or you could have surgery. But surgery is very risky and you might not—*"

"*I'll have it,*" Tanyaradzwa interrupted.

Her father slid his phone into his pocket and looked at her.

"*Tanyaradzwa,*" he said sternly, his voice brimming with caution. He looked at the doctor and tried to excuse his daughter. "*You know these little ones these days. We teach them to speak their mind.*"

"*I strongly advise against surgery,*" the doctor continued.

"*Baba, please let me have it,*" *Tanyaradzwa begged, turning to her father and lowering her soft voice.*

He looked at her and scratched the few hairs that made his beard. "Okay . . ." he began. "When . . . ? How much will we need for this?"

The doctor paused for a moment.

"If you insist on surgery, ummm . . . don't worry about the fees for now; let's focus on getting her better. We could do this at General Hospital. That way your costs would be lower since it is not a private hospital like this one."

Tanyaradzwa looked at her father. Disappointment showed on his face. They both knew the trouble with public hospitals and strikes. The private hospital would have been better. But his business was in trouble and they didn't have enough money.

He nodded.

"If we are going to do the surgery, I would like for us to do it quickly. Perhaps next week?"

She circled a date on her calendar, scribbled something else into the file, and looked up.

"But I would like you to take these in the meantime, Tanyaradzwa. They should help with the pain and nausea. I'm afraid there's not much I can do about the fatigue."

33

Shamiso waited for the bus, wondering what she would tell her mother. Was there a logical reason for a fifteen-year-old to be suspended? That could be a tough one. She didn't know if she could hide the incredible sense of relief she felt at being temporarily dismissed from school.

The matron had wasted no time at all and taken her straight to the principal. She wondered if her mother would understand. Would she sympathize for the way that the principal had looked at her in disgust at the thought of a young woman smoking?

She imagined how angry her mother would be. And worse, how disappointed her father would have been.

Her legs were tired from all the standing and waiting for the bus. It had been an hour, at least. There were no formal schedules, especially given the fuel shortages. She pulled her bag closer to the bus stop and leaned her weight on the pole.

There was hardly any sign of life on the highway. The sun drank the moisture from her skin. She took off her blazer and spread it across her legs. It was the first time in a while her arms had been left bare. Her fingers gently rubbed away the sting of the sun.

The sound of an engine erupted, hissing from afar. She threw herself to her feet. She could see the bus lurching speedily in her direction. It looked packed. She dragged her bag closer to the edge of the road and waved for the bus to stop.

"Is there space?" she called as it pulled in.

The driver laughed. "Mfana, are you going to Harare or not?"

"Is there space?" she repeated. The passengers in the front griped, waving their fists while the driver changed gear and started easing the bus away from the curb. In a panic, Shamiso jumped on and stood behind the driver, close to the front. The bus shook her around as it moved.

"There's no fuel and you're busy worrying about a seat? Why are you even going to Harare? You're running away from school, aren't you?" the bus driver complained bitterly. "Parents are working hard in these difficult times for kids like you to go partying?"

Another passenger joined in. "Ah, mukwasha, you know, children these days don't appreciate the struggle we go through for them to have a decent education!"

"What difference does it make anyway? All the teachers are striking because the government isn't paying them. She's probably better off going home." The comment surfaced from the middle of the bus and was met with dismissive clicks and mumbles from some of the older people. Shamiso craned her neck, trying to see who had said that. It didn't help that the contribution had come from a young man, who looked like he should have been in school himself.

"They're so ungrateful! You'd think with things the way

they are, she'd be there at school, but look at her!" An old woman by the window seat made her passionate contribution, perfectly aware that it takes a whole bus to raise a child.

Shamiso looked at the old woman in confusion. She didn't know what she had done wrong. All she had wanted to know was whether there was a vacant seat on the bus!

34

Shamiso sat on the two-stepped ledge outside the little cottage she was supposed to call home. The door was locked and her mother was nowhere in sight. She racked her brain, trying to come up with a believable story. Her stomach was demanding attention and she had no food, so she lay her head on her bag and slipped into a nap.

"Shamiso?" her mother exclaimed.

Shamiso jumped, wondering where her mother had come from. She had not heard her at all.

Her mother stood there, keys in her hand, waiting for a response. She had grown smaller. Her cheekbones were sharper than Shamiso remembered.

"You cut your hair?" Shamiso asked.

"What are you doing home?" her mother countered.

Shamiso looked away nervously. There was a man standing with her mother. She stared at him suspiciously. Who was he and what was he doing here?

"Umm, they said something about my fees not being up to date," she said, her brow tightening and her eyes fixed on the stranger. She recognized him from somewhere. "Who's this?" she asked.

"Oh, this is Jeremiah." Her mother's voice grew quiet. "He worked with your father. You might remember him from the funeral."

Yes! She remembered him talking to her mother with his hat lowered to his chest. They had been engrossed. Shamiso glared at the stranger for a minute longer; then without another word, she picked up her bags and headed into the house. Somehow he made her angry. The man had done nothing, but his presence made her rage.

The two of them followed her in. She dumped her bags next to the bed and stared at herself in the broken mirror in the corner.

"Tell me what happened," her mother said, standing by the edge of the bed. Shamiso could see her mother's knuckles in the mirror. The skin was peeling slightly, possibly from all the laundry she was being paid to wash in other people's houses.

"I . . . I tried to tell the principal that we paid all my fees, but she wouldn't listen . . ." Shamiso began.

Her mother listened as her daughter's tongue ran wild.

"Did you show her the receipt?" she asked softly.

Shamiso nodded and continued on her rampage of lies. She watched her mother for a reaction, desperate for her to believe her and quell her guilt and shame.

"I don't understand why your principal was so unreasonable," her mother sighed at last.

Shamiso tried to conceal her smile; her mother had bought her story!

"I also don't understand why after being so unreasonable

with fees that you clearly proved that you had paid, she was also cruel enough to suspend you for smoking."

Shamiso's fingers raced to her neck, scraping at it desperately as she tried to silence the itch.

35

Paida sat on her bed, staring at the yellow envelope she had carried from school. She felt obliged to protect her father against whatever those papers meant. She looked at them spread out on her bed, scratching her head and pacing around in her room. The writing itself seemed as though it had been created to deceive. Only the first few paragraphs were legible. She ran her eyes over them for the hundredth time.

All evidence points to the minister. I've even spoken to one of the farm owners. We have proof Jeremiah!

The problem was that this hardly explained anything to Paida. She sighed in frustration.

The gate hummed as it rolled open. She could hear it from her room. Paida rushed to the window and watched a train of cars drive into the yard. She grabbed the envelope and scurried down the stairs. She stood by the end of the staircase, staring at the door to her father's study.

Her brother sat in the living room, watching television.

She held the envelope close to her chest. The sound of men laughing outside drifted into the house.

Her father did not like to be disturbed when he had guests. The rule was always that the kids stay out of his way when he was working.

She peeped through the window to see if he was still outside. He did not take kindly to people in his study. She glanced at the envelope one last time before leaving it on her father's desk. As she headed out of the room, she bumped into him in the doorway with a train of men behind him. He did not say anything; he simply looked at her, his eyes heavy with disapproval. She smiled nervously and skittered out. The door clicked as he shut it behind her.

She could see her brother as he shuffled TV channels, boredom written all over him. She sat on the sofa close to him, curled up into a ball.

"You were in Mr. Hyde's office?" Her brother looked shocked. They had started calling him Jekyll and Hyde because of his unpredictable nature. Paida peeped over her shoulder. Her brother shook his head and waved the remote in the air, offering it to her but she didn't take it. She glanced yet again at the closed door of her father's study. She knew whatever they were doing in there must be to do with the power-sharing deal between the political parties. But she didn't know anything beyond that. Most of her knowledge came from the news. But what if they were now talking about what was in the envelope?

"What are you going to do with the farm Dad got you?" she asked her brother curiously.

Her brother shrugged. "I don't know. I have a guy selling the tractors and fertilizers already though. Dad's lost it if he *thinks I'll become a farmer."* He continued flicking through channels.

Paida's stomach churned. *"You don't care that that farm was a big tea estate before?"*

Her brother chuckled. *"I'm not the one who took it from its owners."*

Paida turned her head in the direction of her father's study again. Whatever was happening in that room seemed to be taking forever. When the door finally opened, her heart sprang at the same time as her feet. Her brother looked puzzled. The men continued to speak as they headed out of the room. Her feet carried her to her father, a frown on her face.

"Paida," he said sharply.

She waited to hear his response. Would he do anything about the information in the envelope? Would he ask where she got it from?

"What did I say about being disturbed when I have company?"

Her brother watched her as she stood there, nervous and confused.

Paida shuffled across and glimpsed her father's desk through the open door. His briefcase sat on top of the envelope. He had not yet read it!

"I'm sorry, Dad," she said, before quickly scurrying back, leaving the letter for whoever might find it. Maybe he did not want to talk about it in front of his friends.

As she turned away, she caught a glimpse of the helper entering the study with her brushes and brooms. With her back turned, Paida could hear her humming, unaware that she was arranging the mess on her father's desk, sweeping up all the letters and envelopes, and taking them to be posted.

36

Heat simmered under Shamiso's feet. The days had been peeling away like old snakeskin. She had only been back for a few days since being suspended, but it felt like it had already been a year. She was realizing to her shame that the challenges of boarding-school life were nothing compared to the naked reality at home.

She had been in the queue since morning. It was now noon. Her stomach grumbled in protest. Food was scarce. She knew almost all of the people around her were suffering from the same plight. The queue had become a common ground for everyone: the teacher, the lawyer, the gardener.

Things were crooked, a sad sort of topsy-turvy. A few weeks back, supplies in the stores had been plentiful. It seemed that Rhodesville had gotten stuck in a nightmare overnight, far from its normal suburban comforts with stores full of supplies and people at their usual hustle and bustle. Not so long ago, the country had been known as the breadbasket of Africa. Now it stood in the aftermath of what seemed like the work of a deadly disease that had furrowed its way to the heart of the country, leaving a trail of turmoil.

A plump woman stood in front of her, holding her sleeping baby. The child lay peacefully in its mother's arms, completely oblivious to what was happening in the world. Shamiso envied the oblivion. Growing up was a tiresome task.

"Excuse me, this queue is for bread, right?" she asked the woman. To her horror, the woman shrugged. Shamiso narrowed her eyes. How could the woman not know why she was in a queue? But then again, neither did she. Shamiso wondered what she would have been doing if she was at school. Part of her longed to be among other teens, sharing in the despair of study time rather than standing in a queue. She glanced at her phone. She had another missed call from Tanyaradzwa. She shoved it into her pocket, as though hiding it would make it go away.

She still could not bring herself to reply to any of her texts or answer her calls. As soon as her phone showed that it was Tanyaradzwa calling, the cycle would begin. The image of blood trickling down Tanyaradzwa's nose while the mbira tumbled to the floor; the memory of her own father's beat-up face in that silk box . . .

The queue had barely moved since she had joined it. All she could see from where she stood was a truck with its back doors open, packed with boxes. A man in overalls sat inside, fighting off the impatient crowd. Shamiso did not understand what was going on. Why weren't they just selling the bread, or whatever it was? But the man in the truck seemed to insist that the boxes be unloaded first, but it was unclear why it hadn't been emptied already. Shamiso didn't think it looked as if there was any bread in there.

Joining a queue had become an adventure, the people unsure what the queue was for, and the shop owners the guardians of a secret they were reluctant to disclose.

An old man stood a few heads away from her, shouting at any outsiders trying to cut ahead.

"You think I won't have bread today? You are joking!" he called.

She closed her eyes and breathed out slowly. She had to remain calm. Her neck itched. The heat gushed hot air in her face. It was all too much!

Suddenly two ladies hurried in front of her. They glanced back and moved in closer to the plump lady, careful to conceal whatever information they wanted to share. One of them held a package, wrapped carefully in a newspaper. Shamiso tilted her head slowly, trying to read it.

"Imi Mai Thandi, they're selling sugar next door," one of the ladies whispered, glancing at Shamiso to make sure she could not hear anything. She rolled her eyes. There was barely any personal space between them so of course she could hear what they were saying.

"It's sugar, Mai Thandi," the other lady insisted, her eyes twinkling at the thought.

"But I'm already standing in this queue," the plump lady answered, rocking her sleeping baby.

"The manager told me they'll be announcing it soon. If we go now before a queue forms, we can get a few packets."

The plump lady hesitated. Shamiso smiled. Sugar was such a sneaky temptation. After all, was it not a bag of sugar that had ushered colonization into the country?

"Did you say there's sugar?" someone else piped up.

The ladies immediately started for the store next door.

Within seconds, everything was chaos. The queue dismantled as the crowd dispersed. The plump lady's child broke into sobs as the woman tried to maneuver herself to the front of the new queue, insisting that she had heard the news first.

Shamiso stood there paralyzed, the painful shrieks of the child ringing in her ears.

The queue had now moved next door. Only four people were left ahead of Shamiso, including the old shouting man. She shuffled closer to the front. In no time at all, she had made it. She watched the old man in front of her pull out his wad of notes, licking his lips as though he would devour the bread right away.

"After I take this home, my wife will definitely know that I am the man of the house today!" He grinned, handing his money to the teller, who in exchange gave him a large packet of crisps.

"Where's the bread?" he protested.

"Move along, old man!" the teller called out as he waved him away. The old man left begrudgingly, muttering to himself. Shamiso watched this exchange in bewilderment. She glanced over at the queue next door and watched as people left the store with loaves of bread.

"I would like some bread, please," she said.

The teller looked at her lazily. "And I want a holiday in the Bahamas. This line is for crisps! If you don't want them, we'll give you back your money."

Shamiso swallowed hard. She picked up a packet of crisps. She had been in this queue for more than an hour so of course she wanted them. She just would have appreciated it more if they had also had bread!

37

A week had passed with Tanyaradzwa's mother away. This time she had been the one who had left the country for work—and the one who could buy a few groceries while she was there.

Tanyaradzwa sat out on the veranda, soaking in the air and waiting for her mother's return. The gardener watered the lawn. The smell of heated grass rose as water poured from the hose onto the parched lawn. It seemed as though he was putting out a fire. But this was the situation. The water shortages were increasing. At least they had a borehole, unlike most people.

Tanyaradzwa flicked on her phone to check the time. Her mother would be home any minute. She glanced at it again, disappointed that Shamiso still had not replied to any of her messages. Perhaps their friendship had only been temporary; it was possible! Perhaps she had mistaken their conversations for something more. Perhaps Shamiso, like everyone else, only saw her as a ticking time bomb.

Her father's Range Rover arrived at the gate and honked.

They were back. The gardener dropped the hose and raced to open the gate. The car drove in and halted in front of the house. Tanyaradzwa stood up and dragged herself to the pillar at the entrance to the veranda.

"Tanyaradzwa," her mother called, arms open wide and heading straight for her. She swallowed her daughter in her embrace. At the same time, their helper headed for the car, peeped into the back and grinned. The trunk of the car brimmed with loaves of bread.

Tanyaradzwa looked at her mother and smiled. "I feel strong, Mama," she said.

Her mother looked at her and nodded lightly.

"I really do," Tanyaradzwa insisted, her voice beginning to shake.

Her mother gripped her by the waist and kissed her on the forehead.

38

Shamiso walked through the gate. The long wait for bread had tired her. In spite of her debacle with the crisps earlier, luck had pitied her and sent bread her way. Who would have known bread could be so priceless? It was hardly one of her favorite things, but somehow it now felt absolutely vital to have. The loaves had been rationed though. The shop owner, thinking he was a paid version of Mother Teresa, had insisted that each customer only take one loaf of bread, to allow everyone to get a share.

The stress of the day kept piling up. She could hear voices in the house. The thought of a visitor in their cottage annoyed her. She quickened her step, eager to find out who it was. She leaned in at the door and listened.

"She's only a little girl," she heard her mother say. "Things like this are not for little girls. It's not how we do things."

"It *should* be how we do things! Do you think when this comes out anyone will care that there are children out there? It's better if we tell her now, ourselves, in a way she will understand."

"That will not happen because it will not come out. You know what would happen if it did. I won't say anything, and neither will you."

Shamiso frowned, her mind spiraling. She immediately pushed open the door of the little cottage and headed in. Papers were scattered everywhere! Her mother sat in the middle of the mess. Jeremiah sat with his back facing Shamiso. Her eye spotted a yellow envelope on the floor next to Jeremiah.

She walked into the cottage slowly.

"Where did you get that?"

Jeremiah turned and began to speak.

"Jeremiah!" her mother cautioned sharply. The man went silent. Shamiso flinched.

"Mom, what's going on?" she said, her voice held tight in her throat.

Jeremiah glanced at her mother, who remained quiet for a while.

"Why don't you go on and make some tea and bread?" her mother suggested.

Shamiso scowled. She could not believe it. All her mother cared about was bread? When it was more than obvious that she was hiding something. The lump in Shamiso's throat tightened. The hand that held the bread shook gently. She tried to hold herself together.

"Shamiso, did you hear me?" her mother asked softly.

Shamiso blinked, then flung the bread at a startled Jeremiah before charging out of the cottage and slamming the door on her way, crisps tight in her hand.

39

Shamiso stepped out of the kombi as it docked at the Fourth Street bus terminus. The conductor handed her the "many" dollars that made up her change and she shoved them into her pocket. The road was close to chaotic, with kombi drivers making it clear that they owned the streets. She stood completely still, staring at the distant vision of the Eastgate Mall towers.

Her father had spoken of his many meet-cutes there and his attempts to charm young women before he met her mother. It had been called the Sunshine City; Harare— the city that never slept. Her father had told her that in Harare dreams flew in the air, which shimmered with endless possibilities. She remembered his narration of how the city of Salisbury had been renamed after independence and how proud he had been when the newspaper agency had given him the opportunity to write about the end of the war.

"It was a big job for a young reckless boy like me. But it was Sunshine City. Anything was possible! And of course I

would never have said no. I had to write it because taivapo—
we were there!" His voice had gleamed with excitement.

She stood by the edge of the terminus wondering if that
sunshine her father had felt would ever return. She watched
a woman under an umbrella with tomatoes laid out neatly in
front of her fan herself energetically. The woman leaned on a
big pole with the sign that read "No hawkers allowed."

Shamiso wiped her brow. The sun still stung, but her mela-
nin had adjusted and her skin had toughened up along with
everyone else's. She felt a strange warmth. Maybe the stories her father had told her were starting to thaw her heart.
She moved quickly, careful not to get herself knocked over.
The queues of passengers waiting to get into kombis were
ridiculous. It was hardly rush hour yet. There must have been
petrol shortages again. She crossed the road and stood on the
pedestrian island, giving way to the speeding cars.

Her mind was busy. Her mother seemed to be spend-
ing more and more time with Jeremiah. He had just come
from nowhere, claimed to have worked with her father and
attained an audience for himself. Her mother didn't seem to
miss her father; she was doing just fine without him. It was as
though everyone had forgotten he had ever existed. She swallowed hard, trying to push down the lump in her throat. As
always it seemed that whenever her thoughts were a blur, her
mind went to Tanyaradzwa.

She pulled out her phone and then pushed it back into her
pocket just as fast. The loss still lingered. She wished she had
someone to talk to. She wondered if her friends in Slough
even remembered her. How could they have abandoned her
in such tough times? She scratched her neck. Maybe that's
what Tanyaradzwa felt. Her stomach turned.

The cars buzzed past her and came to a halt in front of the traffic light. She looked around. The light shone a bright red.

She stood by the edge of the road. Too much was happening in her head. The frustration with her mother sat in her stomach, but at the same time she couldn't erase that look of disappointment in her mother's eyes when she had come home from school. The image of those hands that had worked tirelessly to pay her fees. And then there was her failure as a friend . . .

She stood there dazed, unsure why she had come here or where she was going. She didn't know anyone in town. The queue of cars began to disperse. She turned to the traffic light. It had turned green. Her feet entered the road blindly, crossing the road toward the garage. Screeching sounds hauled her back to reality. She caught sight of her right hand on the bonnet of a black jeep.

The driver jumped out.

"What the hell is wrong with you, man!"

Shamiso stared at her trembling hands. She was unsure what had just happened. A crowd of people from the pavement began to form around her. Shamiso checked to see if she had been hurt, but she could not see any blood. She glanced at the driver.

"You?" she gasped.

"You!" Tinotenda replied, stepping back in astonishment.

40

Tanyaradzwa's father sat on the couch opposite her, his fingers punching away on his laptop as though his life depended on it. Her mother was in her bedroom, scrubbing again. She did that a lot lately. It seemed to help her cope.

The generator hummed in the background, relieving them from ZESA's Houdini acts. Tanyaradzwa lay on the couch, disregarding the heat and covering herself with a quilt. The bread and cheese her mother had brought her sat on the coffee table, untouched. Her eyes blinked lazily at the television. Her ears picked up the sound but she was beginning to give in to sleep.

An unexpected song blared from the television.

"Mai Tanyaradzwa! Mai Tanyaradzwa! It's starting!" her father hissed.

Tanyaradzwa's eyes flipped open. She tried to sit up. Baba would find it disrespectful if she didn't.

A procession of uniformed soldiers marched musically across the screen in their green berets, facing sideways and holding a rifle at an angle with both arms. Her mother raced *down the stairs and leaned on the couch. Tanyaradzwa turned just in time to see the excitement on her face.*

The two political parties had been at loggerheads for years. It was a miracle they were even in the same room, uniting to form an inclusive government. People had died for this. Her own teacher, Mr. Mpofu, had been badly injured. Tanyaradzwa's eyes shifted to her father. He sat on the edge of his seat, nervously rubbing his leg, watching the television intently.

They all went quiet as they watched the president and the newly inaugurated prime minister, a member of the opposition party, shake hands and agree to work together. The last time the country had had both posts filled was back in 1980, right after independence.

"This might be promising," her mother said, dancing slightly. It was the first time in months there had been a glimmer in her eyes. It was subtle, but Tanyaradzwa noticed it all the same. The hope was there, but like a dying fire it needed to be gently blown into.

41

The crowd had grown. Shamiso felt exposed.

"We should call the police," someone suggested.

Both Shamiso and Tinotenda panicked.

"Get in the car," he hissed at her.

"I'm okay," she protested.

"Get in the car!" he barked again.

She scurried toward the passenger door and slid in. He drove off, breaking up the crowd in the process. He watched through the rearview mirror as they waved their fists. His heart was racing.

"What are you doing here anyway? Shouldn't you be at school or something?"

Tinotenda turned to her, eyebrow raised. "Shouldn't *you* be in school? Oh wait, I forgot, you're not allowed there!"

Shamiso looked out of the window.

Tinotenda's eyes returned to the road. He glanced back at Shamiso, discomfited by the silence. "Okay . . . Mom! It's the school break. Gee, *bruh*, ease up a little, will you?"

Shamiso kept her gaze out of the window, watching the cars rush past as Tinotenda drove on.

"How far is the class on math? Is Mr. Mpofu still coming to class?" Shamiso asked after a while.

Tinotenda glanced at her. "Ummm . . . we were told that Mr. Mpofu has been missing since that rally he went to near the school. People think that he got himself in trouble because of his political opinions." His voice was quiet.

Shamiso drew down the window and breathed in deeply. She knew what missing meant.

She looked at him suspiciously, then returned her gaze to outside the window. Her phone vibrated. Tinotenda glanced over at her and she covered the phone so he couldn't see the screen. Tanyaradzwa's mother had been calling all morning. She could not bring herself to answer the phone. In case . . .

Shamiso stared at the screen, ashamed yet shackled by fear.

"Where are you taking me?" she asked, turning to face him.

"But for reals, you know I could have run you over back there, right?"

"Tinotenda . . ." Shamiso breathed in, tying down the lumps of anger that were beginning to build up in her voice. "I said, where are you taking me?"

"Just relax, okay? We're going to get a drink."

Shamiso sniffed the air. "You were drinking?" Her voice trembled. "You could have killed me."

Tinotenda kept his eyes on the road. "Stop the car!" she insisted. He didn't react. She shoved him in the shoulder, forcing his hands to jerk and the car to swerve.

"Dude! What the hell is wrong with you? Are you trying to get us killed?" Tinotenda pulled his car from the fast lane, getting ready to turn. "It's just a little alcohol, for crying out loud. It's no big deal! Don't act like you don't drink!" He turned the car into the Parkade.

"I'm underage."

"And yet you smoke," he said with a smirk.

She kept her eyes on him as he came to a halt, undid his seatbelt and got out of the car.

"Listen, I know it must be hard with Tanya being ill . . ."

Shamiso looked at him for a while, face wound up in a knot.

"I mean, I barely know you, but I'm guessing things aren't exactly easy right now . . ." He stopped as Shamiso looked away.

"Listen, all I'm saying is that a beer will relax you a little. C'mon."

Shamiso thought for a while.

"They won't allow us to drink anyway. Not without ID."

Tinotenda pulled something out of his pocket. "I'm sure the bartender will understand that I changed my name to Andrew Jackson," he said, waving around a US twenty-dollar note. They had begun flooding the black market. The US dollar was much more reliable and didn't have an infinite reserve of unpredictable zeros. Shamiso bit her lip. She had nowhere else to go. She would have preferred a cigarette, but at this point any sort of distraction would have to do.

"If I decide to drink, it'll just be one beer."

"Of course." He winked.

42

Tanyaradzwa stared again at the helicopter fan on the ceiling. She could feel the soft beats of her heart. Little traces of fear threaded their way through the darkness. It was all unpredictable now.

She glanced at her phone again. Shamiso had not been in touch.

The door creaked slightly. Her mother popped her head around.

"You all right?"

"Yes, Mama."

"Are you sure you want to go ahead with this surgery?" Her mother did not hide her desperate hope that her daughter would reconsider.

Tanyaradzwa kept her voice breezy. "I'll be all right." She wished her parents would conceal their fears.

Her mother stood there a while longer. "Are you going to ask your friend to come see you? I haven't been able to get her on the phone."

Silence.

"*Maybe she's scared too?*"

"*That is no excuse!*" *Tanyaradzwa said in her broken whisper. Her mother came in and closed the door. Streaks of moonlight made it in, sneaking through the open spaces between the leaves of the tree outside.*

"*It's okay to be hurt when you feel like people have forgotten about you, or when it feels like they've chosen to live without you,*" *her mother said, rubbing her daughter's arm.*

Tanyaradzwa kept her head low, tears flowing freely down her cheeks.

"*It's okay to be upset. But, darling, maybe if you accept that people are people and they're made out of a lifetime of mistakes and fears, maybe you'd find yourself a lot more gracious.*"

Her mother paused in the stolen light, then slowly drew her crying daughter into her embrace.

43

The sky shone bright and clear again, harboring wisps of clouds. Shamiso's head hammered, throbbing at her temples and threatening to break through her forehead. The one drink she had intended to have the day before had turned into several. Everything about the previous night was a blur. She hardly remembered how she had made it back home. But whatever had happened had not impressed her mother at all.

She had barely said anything, but her silence spoke loudly. In fact, she had woken up early, switched on the radio and then put a CD of Oliver Mtukudzi's timeless voice on repeat at a blasting fury of volume.

The monotony of the song mocked her, hurting her ears, like rubbing Styrofoam against the wall. Nothing made the pain stop, not even holding her head. She lifted it again and stared at the radio, eyes twitching.

Mtukudzi went on singing. "Help me Lord I'm feeling low!"

Shamiso rubbed her temples and looked down at her feet

before heading to the window. Jeremiah stood there, talking to her mother in hushed tones. Shamiso watched his hands making gestures, and his head turning back and forth like cautious prey. She wondered what he thought he was giving away with those gestures.

Her mother's hands reached up to rub her eyes. Shamiso watched her rocking herself gently as she stood there. Jeremiah lingered silently for a while, then put his hand on her shoulder. Shamiso looked away. Jeremiah looked far too cozy with her mother. Her father would not approve!

Before she knew it, her hand was tugging at the door.

"Of course I understand this is sensitive, but I can't keep this story to myself. I've already organized to meet with a journalist who will run the story. People must know. Just as Shamiso must . . ." She heard Jeremiah's murmur. They both went quiet as she approached.

Jeremiah fidgeted nervously.

"I need money," Shamiso said to her mother, eyes fixed on Jeremiah.

Her mother pulled her face into a knot.

"For a movie or a burger; something!" Shamiso insisted. "Since you're clearly busy, I think I have to get out of the house—"

"Shamiso," Jeremiah interrupted, "I think you should know that when your father came here he was chasing after a story."

Shamiso felt her eyes turn to knives. She turned to her mother, whose face was shouting for Jeremiah to refrain from whatever he was doing. Jeremiah kept his gaze fixed on the ground and continued.

"Your mother will tell you in detail, but your father

discovered that one of the ministers was giving farms to his friends and auctioning them off to businessmen who could afford to bid more for them than actual qualified farmers. I think he suspected that his life was in danger and he wanted me to tell this story to the world because it was sent to me in an envelope addressed in his handwriting."

Shamiso's heart began to race, her mind drowning out every other noise. The envelope! It had been in her satchel and she had not read it. Her father's story! She had not flipped a single page!

"Jeremiah, please leave!" her mother insisted, shattering the silence.

Shamiso stared at Jeremiah, her body a raw wound, her flesh seared.

"This story will be in the papers tomorrow; I am already making sure of it. But I didn't want you to find out from a newspaper."

"Leave now!" Her mother shouted, her veins popping out of her skin.

Jeremiah quietly nodded and headed out toward the gate.

Shamiso waited for her mother to say more but she only rocked back and forth, incapable of speech. How could she have kept all this from her? The lump danced uncomfortably in her throat.

Suddenly, her mother came back to life and said confidently, "I have a job in Chishawasha Hills today."

"Is what Jeremiah said true?" Shamiso gasped, choking on her anger.

The bags under her mother's eyes darkened. "You will come with me. I need help."

Shamiso stood there, unable to breathe and shackled by

rage. She could not understand why her mother was carrying on as though the conversation had not happened.

"You want money for a movie?" Her mother chuckled. "You think I slave like this so that you can watch movies?"

Shamiso said nothing.

44

A cluster of gray clouds gathered above them as they walked up the incline on Pine Street. Shamiso tried not to think how the gray skies reminded her of England.

Her legs began to protest. It was a long walk from Rhodesville. She did not want to go to work. She wondered if this qualified as child labor. Her mother walked slightly in front of her, a small handbag under her arm. She seemed to be enjoying the wind as it cooled her face.

The environment had already changed.

Somewhere along the way, the yards had grown bigger. The lawns had become greener, whistling sprinklers raining water onto them. Trees stood proud, dancing in the rich breeze and blowing cold air at Shamiso. She rubbed the goosebumps on her arms.

A black Hummer passed them. Shamiso watched it turn into a driveway a small distance away. As the gate slid open, two Labradors shot out barking. Shamiso froze. She did not even blink, keeping steady and praying that they would not come any closer.

Her mother continued on. The Labradors raced in their direction.

Shamiso's legs backed up. She held her breath. She had heard they could smell fear. But fear oozed out of her and stained the air she breathed. If they could smell fear, she was sure she was about to die. She watched the beasts heading toward her with their teeth out. Her pace quickened, her body still facing them as she walked backward. She had heard they didn't appreciate running. Who came up with these things?

"Shumba! Come back here, boy!" a white man beckoned, finally coming out of the Hummer. The dogs magically turned into puppies and raced back to their owner, tails wagging high in the air. Shamiso breathed out.

Her mother looked back and giggled. Shamiso scratched her neck. Her mother had not smiled much, let alone giggled, since their dreadful loss. It was just a shame Shamiso could not bring herself to appreciate the humor.

Shamiso marched on, ready to bolt at any time. Her eyes stayed glued to the gate as it slid shut. She continued up the slope. The houses grew fancier, the yards even bigger. For a moment she wondered if the drought had reached this part of the city at all.

"We're here," her mother said at last, confirming the address on her phone. Shamiso fidgeted. Her legs were worn out. She hated the reason they were here.

Her mother pressed the intercom.

"Yes?" A stern voice erupted from the machine.

"Er . . . we . . ." She paused and looked at Shamiso. "I am here to do the laundry?"

Shamiso's eyes shifted to her mother. Somehow, although

she already knew the types of jobs her mother did, it bothered her to hear it said out loud. Hearing it made it real.

Her mother waited, bent over the intercom. Shamiso glanced at her hands. She wondered how many times she had washed dirty clothes to put food on their table.

Their old life had really vanished. Things were different now. Somehow her complaints about the dietary changes back at school felt trivial all of a sudden.

The other side of the intercom remained quiet. It seemed the voice had disappeared, but just then the gate buzzed open. Mother and daughter walked in.

Before them stood a white mansion surrounded by a colorful flower garden. She watched as two gardeners clipped away on opposite sides of a hedge, shaping it to size. The gardeners paid no attention to them. Shamiso and her mother followed the path to the door. Her mother knocked. They could hear voices in the house. Shamiso looked up nervously. The clouds had disappeared. The sky had become bare again.

The door opened and Shamiso recoiled in horror.

45

The doctor felt Tanyaradzwa's chest for a heartbeat. Tanyaradzwa smiled faintly.

"Everything seems fine. Someone will come get you in a few minutes and take you to the theater. I will be waiting for you there. Do you have any questions?" The doctor wiped her spectacles as she spoke.

Tanyaradzwa smiled again and shrugged.

"Right, see you in a bit then." The doctor got ready to leave.

"It'll be okay, right?" Tanyaradzwa asked in a feeble whisper.

The doctor hesitated. "I will do my very best. You have my word on that. But if you've changed your mind, there are other . . ."

Tanyaradzwa shook her head. The doctor nodded and walked out of the room. As she headed to the theater, she passed by the nurse's desk. The nurse on duty was wearing scrubs and punching something into the computer in front of her.

"Everything in order?" she asked.

"Yes, doctor. You have my word that nothing will go wrong," the nurse promised.

46

Shamiso could not believe it. She wished there was a hole to creep into. She stepped back, chin up and hands folded.

Paida stood by the door, equally dumbstruck.

"What are you doing here?" she asked, fear making her brown skin almost pale.

Shamiso's mother's eyes darted between the two of them.

"I believe you have dirty laundry?" her mother asked, her voice suddenly cold.

Shamiso could just about see the inside of the house. The size of the place was astonishing, decorated elaborately with expensive pieces of furniture.

"You can't be here, Shamiso, you have to go," Paida said as she glanced back into the house.

Humiliation seized her and she began to turn away.

Her mother cleared her throat. "I don't understand. I was asked to come and do some laundry."

"There's no time for this. You have to leave." Paida grabbed Shamiso's arm. "Now!"

Shamiso stood there completely lost. She pulled her hand

away and looked at her mother. She did not understand any of it.

A deep, angry voice floated toward them from inside the house. A sharp back and forth emanated from the background, all muffled and impossible to discern. Paida turned back nervously.

"Make this go away!" a man said as he emerged into view, holding a glass of brandy. Two other men followed behind him.

Shamiso pushed her head forward to see if she could get a better look. Her eyes narrowed.

"Isn't that the minister?" she asked her mother. Her mother's face tightened. "Wait, the minister is your dad?" Shamiso turned to Paida in total shock.

Her mother remained quiet. She stood with her hands folded, nostrils wide and eyes refusing to blink at all.

"Mom," Shamiso whispered. Her mother breathed heavily. Paida trembled with fear, unsure of what to do.

"You *murderer*." Shamiso's mother broke the silence, charging into the house toward the three men. Shamiso watched as her mother pounced. Paida's hands clasped her mouth. The other men wrestled Shamiso's screaming mother away from the minister.

"You killed my husband!" she barked, writhing away from their grip. Shamiso had never seen her mother like this.

"Paida! Who are these people?" the minister shouted, dabbing at the cut on his cheek as the men hauled her mother outside.

"They were supposed to—"

"Get them out of here! Now!"

"You killed my husband!" Shamiso's mother repeated but the words stuck in her throat.

Paida turned to Shamiso. "You really should go."

Shamiso's mother gasped for air as she wiped the tears from her eyes. Her heart shook. She glanced at her horrified daughter. All she had wanted was to tap some reality into the girl, show her how their life had changed. Maybe then she would appreciate school. Maybe she would adjust and the fight within her would rise. But all she had done was crumple in front of her daughter and scare her half to death.

She patted her eyes once more and in a calm voice turned to Shamiso and said, "Let's go."

47

Paida closed the door.

"Do you think it was linked to that envelope?" she asked her father quietly.

"What envelope?" he said, still dabbing at his cheek as he stared into the mirror in the hallway.

"The one I left in your office."

He turned and looked at her, eyes blazing.

"What did I say about my office, Paida? I have told you before—my office is out of bounds."

"But the envelope said something about you taking bribes for farms during the redistribution. I thought I was helping!" she said, her voice rising.

Her father froze. She watched him nervously, unsure if his silence spoke of disapproval.

"What did you say?" he asked, his eyes bulging.

"I found an envelope that girl dropped at school, and it said you were taking bribes and giving stolen farms to your friends."

"And you left it in my office?" he said, heading back into

his office and rummaging through the papers on his desk, recreating the mess that had been there before.

"Where, Paida? Where?" he hissed. "It was probably sent out with the post! Do you know what this could do to us if it falls into the wrong hands?" he raged as he pulled out his phone.

Paida began to explain again, but her father stormed out, heading for his car. She trotted behind him and watched as he sped off. She stood there nervously, wondering what on earth would happen if Mr. Hyde overpowered Dr. Jekyll.

48

The doctor stood in the room, her hands suspended, gloves colored with blood. Tanyaradzwa lay with a tube in her mouth and an oxygen mask over her face. Her throat had been cut into and her bumpy trachea lay exposed.

"Scalpel," said the doctor calmly. The nurse on her right placed the sharp metal object into her steady hand. As her hand moved to the girl's throat the lights in the operating theater suddenly blinked. She stopped and looked at the team of nurses around her.

"Do we have a generator on standby?"

"We should, but I will double-check," one of the nurses said, hurrying out of the room.

The lights normalized. The doctor breathed in her relief. The lights blinked again. And then there it was.

ZESA!

49

Jeremiah sat uneasily in his car, waiting in the parking zone and holding the yellow envelope in his hand. A car stopped next to his and the driver stared at him. Jeremiah looked away nervously and deliberately locked his car doors.

The car drove off. Jeremiah glanced around and turned his wrist to see the time again. Someone knocked on the car window, making him jump.

"Were you followed?" Jeremiah asked, unlocking the door.

"No," the other man said, confused at the question.

"Here, everything is in there," he said, moving to hand over the envelope. The man reached out to get it, but Jeremiah's hesitation held on for a minute longer.

The man pulled out the papers and read through them.

"Muloy had caught a big fish here."

Jeremiah nodded. He felt satisfied with the part he had played for justice, like a load had been lifted from his chest. His friend's life had not been stolen for nothing!

"Make sure it gets out," he pleaded before leaving for home.

50

After everything that had just happened, Shamiso found herself standing at the hospital entrance, unsure whether or not this visit was a good idea. She thought of her mother, and the pain that had been written on her face. It resonated with the panic Shamiso felt inside. What would the consequences be for what her mother had just done?

She had clarity about only one thing: she needed to be there for Tanyaradzwa. The same way she wished her friends back home had been there for her. Fear rode along and stood next to her, its hand in hers.

Nurses and doctors rushed in and out of rooms. The hospital did not seem to have been hit much by the strike. She scratched her neck and swallowed. It had been a while since she had smoked. With hardly any money from her mother, it had become virtually impossible to buy cigarettes.

Shamiso wondered if Tanyaradzwa would even speak to her. After all, there had been so many missed calls and unanswered messages. Her feet carried her forward. A nurse sat there, one hand to her ear as she tended to calls.

"Yes?" the nurse asked.

"I'm looking for Tanyaradzwa Pfumojena," Shamiso stuttered. The nurse balanced the phone on her shoulder as she typed into her desktop.

"Are you family?"

Shamiso paused for a minute, then nodded. The nurse seemed uninterested anyway. She juggled both the phone and the monitor.

"Room 106," she said distractedly.

As Shamiso walked to the ward, she worried that her chest might burst open from the drumming of her heart. The walls of the corridors were painted with smells of strong medicine and spirits. Her eyes searched for the right room number. The closer she got, the faster her heart became until she could almost see the room from where she stood.

As the nurses and doctors came and went, her eyes drifted to the water dispenser in the hallway. An overwhelming thirst caught up with her. She walked to the dispenser and gulped down a cup of water. It gave her brain freeze. She stared at the empty plastic cup and found herself pushing the tap for another glass. She took two giant sips and headed for the door.

PART FIVE

the following week

51

Nothing in this world is for keeps. And although Shamiso still failed to say the words out loud, they had slowly become her silent mantra.

She sat in the kitchen head in her hands, tears seeping from her eyes. She had come home to the news that Jeremiah's son had called. Jeremiah had been beaten to death and thrown in a ditch close to his house. Some men had been lingering near his house the previous night. Jeremiah's son suspected that they must have attacked him as he set out early for work—he'd left while it was still dark because his car had run out of petrol and he had to use public transport, which was not so easy lately with the petrol problems. People had discovered him only later that morning.

After wiping her eyes, Shamiso took a deep breath and sat up straight. It was only then that she noticed the newspaper on the white plastic chair beside her. The headline revealed the secret that the envelope had carried all this time.

Muloy Exposes Corrupt Minister from the Grave

Jeremiah had died for that headline, for the front-page news. Fear hissed in her ear, reminding her that everyone was dropping like flies. But how could she allow herself to be afraid? After the courage Jeremiah had shown by fighting for the truth—and her father's courage in dying because of it?

The silence in the house was unbearable. Images of Tanyaradzwa in tubes and surrounded by beeping machines shook her. How could she not be afraid, when death was so real? It had only been two days, but fear kept her from calling. Maybe if she stayed away, the loss would pardon her. Because how could she lose something she no longer had?

She pressed her hands on her head and searched desperately for the hope Tanyaradzwa had held so vehemently. Tears drooled from her eyes and sobs erupted within her. The lump slipped back into her throat. She needed it all to stop!

She grabbed the bottle holding the candle and smashed it to the ground in a bid to discharge her anger. The wick snuffed out. The room welcomed the blooming darkness. Her senses settled and she groped around for the box of matches, yelping as a sharp, thick piece of broken glass dug right through her palm. And as the blood oozed out, flowing down her hand, onto her shin and dripping to her foot, she fainted.

52

Shamiso opened her eyes, her senses flooded by the strong smell of disease and medicine.

She pulled herself up. Her mother stood a short distance away, talking to a nurse in a white uniform with a navy blue jersey. She tried to move her hand where the glass had mercilessly forced its way in. She winced in pain, realizing that it was wrapped in spirit-soaked bandages. The cut must have been deep.

The man in the bed next to her coughed. He had a tube of oxygen stuck in his nose and his mouth moved as though chewing at something. The curtains purred as a nurse pulled them around the bed of the old woman across from her.

A loud screech broke from behind the curtain. Shamiso's bed rocked. Another nurse, who was pushing a trolley stacked with needles, had accidentally bumped into her bed.

Her mother and the nurse with the blue jersey were walking toward her. A soft gratitude settled on her. Her mother had always been there for her, through everything.

Shamiso could also see her grandmother heading for the

bed. Her tiny black handbag sat squashed by her hand, in her armpit; her dhuku was lightly tied as always. Shamiso wondered when she had arrived. The nurse grabbed the corner of the curtain hanging on the rail and pulled it around her bed. Shamiso couldn't breathe.

"Mom, let's go home," she begged.

"Not just yet, mwanangu. The nurse will give you something for the pain and then, after they stitch you up, they'll monitor you overnight." Her mother sounded worn out. Her grandmother stood next to her mother, lips downturned, both hands holding the handle of her bag and head shaking. Shamiso watched the nurse with the trolley stretch her latex glove and pull a gigantic needle from a sealed plastic envelope on her tray. The nurse flicked the tip of the syringe, making droplets of medicine land on Shamiso's skin. The girl's back trickled with sweat. The nurse now drew closer, clutched her wrist, and held it tightly. Shamiso's eyebrows bunched up. She bit her lip and followed the pointy needle as it headed her way. And as the saying goes, when life hands you lemons, you scream your lungs out!

53

Shamiso sat at the back of the house, leaning against the walls of the old cottage. Her palm both itched and ached from the previous day. Her chin rested on her knees. When she had been a little girl, her father used to carry her on his shoulders. She remembered how invincible she had felt. But whenever he brought her down, it was always her mother who caught her.

She curled her toes, pulling them away from the creeping traces of the sun. She glanced at her phone. Tanyaradzwa's mother had stopped calling since Shamiso had been to the hospital. She wondered if her friend was all right, but couldn't imagine going back there.

Her blood quivered, trying to convince her that enough time had already been wasted. The oily smell of fried fat cakes came from the house and teased her nostrils. Her grandmother had been staying with them since the "incident."

She heard footsteps as her grandmother emerged.

"Come eat," she said and disappeared almost as quickly as she had appeared.

Shamiso got to her feet and walked into the house. Her

grandmother sat on the floor ready to dig in. A generous number of fat cakes lay on the plate in front of her.

"Wake your mother up," she instructed, fixing her dhuku again and mumbling something to herself.

Shamiso headed for the other room. She softly opened the door and stood there. Her mother was sitting on the bed, staring into nothingness, gently rocking herself. Shamiso walked over and sat by her side, letting her mother feel her presence. Somehow it had all gotten to be too much. Seeing the minister, hearing of Jeremiah's death, reading that paper; her mother must have felt as though she was losing her husband all over again.

Shamiso wondered if the two of them would lose one another too. Her piercing eyes rested on her mother. Tears pushed up against her. She placed her hand on her mother's shoulder.

"Mom, Ambuya says tea's ready," she whispered. Her mother looked at her blankly, then turned her head away and continued rocking.

54

Shamiso walked back to the ward. It had been a few days since she was last here. She wiped her dry mouth and scratched her itchy neck. As she neared the room, she could hear singing. The door was open. She quickened her step, eager to see what was going on.

Tanyaradzwa's band stood around her bed, singing with their heads hung low as though saying farewell before sending her off. Shamiso peeped inside. Gloom colored the room gray. Tanyaradzwa's mother sat in the corner, folded into a neat package of misery. Shamiso could understand how she must feel. She had left that same image at home.

She wondered whether or not to run. It was happening again, just as she had feared, but she could not block out the haunting words of her father, delivered to her by Tanyaradzwa like a message in a bottle. Hope.

She could hear the band starting to walk out and looked to see where she could hide.

"Shamiso?"

She turned. Tinotenda smiled as he walked toward her.

He seemed a little more serious than usual. Shamiso blinked. Tinotenda put his hand on her shoulder.

"We're still going to play at the festival if you want to come. A tribute to Tanya."

Shamiso frowned. "What do you mean, a tribute?"

Tinotenda scratched his head. "Well, let's see what happens."

"Shamiso," she heard a high voice and peered past Tinotenda.

"Paida."

Tinotenda started for the exit. Shamiso crossed her arms.

"What are you doing here?" she stuttered.

Paida looked down for a moment. "Listen, I'm not here to fight with you."

The lump.

The image of her mother as she charged at the minister.

"I'm really sorry about your dad. And . . . and about Tanyaradzwa."

Shamiso frowned but no sarcasm fell from Paida's lips. No horns grew on her forehead either.

"Thanks, but Tanyaradzwa is going to be all right," Shamiso said quietly.

Paida nodded and walked away. Shamiso watched her go. For a little longer than she needed to. Perhaps it was easier than entering the room.

Shamiso stepped into the gloom. Tanyaradzwa lay there asleep, just as she remembered. Face swollen, tubes running to and from her face and body. Little beeps from the machines kept her company. Shamiso looked across the room. Tanyaradzwa's mother was slumped in an armchair next to her daughter's bed, one hand supporting her head as she dozed.

The doctor entered. She glanced at Shamiso and smiled. Then she walked over to the armchair and gently tapped Tanyaradzwa's mother on the shoulder.

She opened her eyes with a start. "I must have fallen asleep."

"That's all right," the doctor said, rubbing her arm. "Can I talk to you for a minute outside, please?"

Tanyaradzwa's mother got up.

"Shamiso! I didn't hear you come in," she said in surprise.

Shamiso opened her mouth but no words came out. She only just managed to smile.

Tanyaradzwa's mother pulled her into an embrace and held her tight for a minute, before following the doctor outside.

Shamiso watched Tanyaradzwa's chest as it moved up and down. What did people do in these situations?

"I'm not sure what to say," she whispered.

She glanced outside. She could hear fragments of what the doctor and Tanyaradzwa's mother was saying.

"Like I said yesterday, we can't keep her for more than a week if she's still in a coma. Unless you can foot the bill . . ."

"I thought you said the surgery went well. That's what you said, isn't it?"

"There were complications during surgery, I will not lie to you . . . Overall everything went well . . . Sometimes patients are simply exhausted and they don't wake up in time. We have four more days."

Shamiso stood up. Four days. Her heart skipped about wildly and her feet wanted to run. Four days! But in the calm of the noise, her father's words echoed, etched into her brain.

She stared her choices in the face.

55

One of the machines hooked to Tanyaradzwa beeped. Shamiso watched the little white light as it skated on the screen, running up and down drawing the green patterns of her heartbeat. Another machine made calculated huffs as though it was a pump someone was playing with. Shamiso's eyes drifted toward the sleeping Tanyaradzwa. Silence seemed most appropriate.

She had to stay. It felt right for her to be sitting in that chair.

"You know, being hooked up to machines is a good way to get out of showering every day."

Shamiso turned in surprise. Tinotenda stood by the door, pretending to be in deep thought.

"It's actually a clever way not to do dishes as well. Except that she's missing all the fun of queuing for bread and stuff," he continued.

A slight smile shone from behind Shamiso's eyes.

Tinotenda shrugged. "Too soon?"

Shamiso remained silent for a few more seconds before breaking into tears of laughter.

56

Shamiso opened the door to the cottage. Her grandmother knelt by a box in the lounge, packing away her father's papers. Her tufty gray hair was uncovered. Shamiso closed the door behind her.

"Good afternoon." She removed her bag from her shoulder.

Her grandmother lifted her head and looked at her. "How is your friend?"

Shamiso shook her head lightly. But this time the fear had let go of her hand. She would be there. She would be a friend. She would be a daughter.

"How is Mom?"

Her grandmother turned in the direction of the bedroom. "Come make yourself useful." She beckoned her over. Shamiso placed her bag on the white chair by the wall and knelt beside her grandmother. They stayed next to each other for a while, in silence, sorting through her father's belongings. Her grandmother would pull each item out of the box, hand it to her, and she would either stack it in the pile to burn, or in the one to keep. All his papers, all his notes. It was time to let them go.

Then her grandmother pulled out the mbira. Shamiso's heart stopped.

"Do you know what this is?" she asked.

Shamiso nodded.

"Did you know I taught your father how to play?"

Shamiso hesitated.

"You don't believe me?" Her grandmother chuckled as she shuffled back and set her bottom on the floor. She put the mbira on her lap and cracked her knuckles. Shamiso watched her fingers as they brushed the keys of the instrument. Her shriveled hands brought the mbira to life. The skin on her fingers had furrowed slightly and her nails were rough and brittle. But strong, just like her father's.

Her grandmother placed the mbira in her hands and put one arm around her. Shamiso could smell the cinnamon stuck to her jersey from the fat cakes she made every morning. The old woman's hands rested lightly on top of hers and she pressed both of their fingers on the keys. Shamiso smiled. Her grandmother's hands had the same soft touch as her father's. The old woman slowly took her hands away.

"Don't stop. Keep going," she said as she stood back up.

"It hurts my fingers though. And I'm no good." Shamiso put the instrument down on the floor.

Her grandmother smiled. "You sound just like your father when he first learned to play."

"Really? I thought he loved the mbira."

"He did," her grandmother said. "But at first he couldn't stand it."

"Then what happened?"

"Well, his father—your grandfather—told him he had a choice to make. He could quit if it was the instrument that was making him miserable. But if it was the learning he was trying to avoid, he would have to toughen up." Shamiso watched the wrinkles tighten as her grandmother smiled. She stared at the mbira and picked it up again. Her fingers started to strum.

"Ambuya, can I ask you something?" she said as she struggled with the keys.

Her grandmother nodded.

"How come you and my dad didn't get along?"

Her grandmother continued arranging things as though she had not heard her, and Shamiso returned to her strumming. A light shadow grazed her feet. She turned her head. Her mother stood by the door. She rested against the frame and stared at Shamiso.

"Keep playing," she said softly.

Shamiso glanced at her grandmother. This lesson had turned out to be longer than she had anticipated. The tips of her fingers burned, but it was worth it. The tune gradually took shape. Her mother watched her, blinking slowly. Her grandmother kept folding and ripping papers.

Then suddenly her grandmother stopped packing and held up a photograph. She turned to Shamiso and her mother and burst out laughing.

"Did your father ever tell you about his bell-bottoms days? He thought he was the most stylish of them all." She handed Shamiso the picture. Shamiso took it and grinned.

"Aren't these bootleg jeans, Ambuya?"

Her grandmother seemed to draw a blank, though she was still smiling.

Shamiso studied the photo. Her father seemed happy, his head back and teeth showing. He stood in front of an old car with Shamiso's mother on his arm, back in the day before most photographs carried color. Once, when Shamiso was nine, she had asked him what it had been like to live in a world where everything was black and white. She could almost hear his laugh in her grandmother's voice.

"He sure loved to laugh," her mother said. She took the picture from Shamiso's hand.

"Yes, he did," her grandmother said.

Shamiso held her breath, watching her mother.

"Even when he wrote about serious things, he always tried to make people laugh."

"You know I still can't agree with his politics, but I've always admired how determined and courageous he was." Her grandmother wiped her eyes. "I only wish we hadn't let our views come between us."

Her mother's face twisted, lines on her forehead forming, tears falling. Shamiso found herself stumbling forward and embracing her. Her grandmother swept in and joined the hug. Shamiso felt the gentle stroke of her grandmother's hand on her back, rubbing both of their backs. Then the old woman stepped aside and switched on the radio.

Due to the evidence found against the minister concerning corruption allegations in line with the land redistribution, he has been dismissed from office by members of parliament. Furthermore, he awaits trial regarding Patrick Muloy's death in the high court. This ends this news bulletin.

57

Shamiso sat in the same armchair she had been in for the past four days, watching Tanyaradzwa as she lay there in the bed. Tanyaradzwa's parents had stepped out for a moment. Shamiso slid her hand into Tanyaradzwa's. Her palms were soft and warm and full of life.

"I have a surprise for you," she said as she pulled her hand away and picked up the mbira. "I don't really believe it either. I used to be rubbish at this. I mean, I'm no musician, but I can play a few songs now. My grandmother has been teaching me." She looked at Tanyaradzwa. The machine beeped. Tanyaradzwa's body was still, her chest moving slowly up and down as it always did.

Shamiso placed the mbira on her lap and started playing. The mbira awoke, the jazzy clicks of the keys sending melody into the room. Tears streamed down her cheeks as she played, and she kept her eyes fixed on Tanyaradzwa, hoping the music had done something.

Nothing . . .

"If you don't wake up now, they're going to unplug you,"

she said, grabbing Tanyaradzwa's lifeless arm. "It's scary to fight, I know that. But you have to try! This can't be how your story ends."

The beeps kept sounding. Fear circled around Shamiso, screeching and croaking. But she would not give up on her friend.

She rubbed her arm gently and waited.

Nothing . . .

She finally resorted to anger.

"You're such a hypocrite! You told me I had to fight and you throw in the towel?"

She felt a tap on her shoulder. Tanyaradzwa's mother stood behind her.

"Shamiso," she said softly. "Can we have a few moments alone with her?"

Shamiso nodded. She picked up her mbira and headed out.

58

Shamiso sat in between her mother and grandmother in the tiny living room. Her grandmother was telling stories about her younger self during the war. She glanced at her mother as she rippled with laughter. Shamiso had not heard that laugh in a long time. She smiled and rested her head on her mother's shoulder.

The midnight news bulletin played on the radio in the background. The clock struck twelve. The last day had officially passed. She stole a glance at her phone.

Still nothing. She wondered how the pain she expected to feel would sting her this time.

The phone rang. Her mother and grandmother stopped talking. They both looked at Shamiso and waited for her to answer. She hesitated, not wanting to hear the bad news.

Her mother picked up the phone and pressed the green button.

"Shamiso." She extended her arm. Shamiso's heart stopped. Her mother smiled. Tears fell from Shamiso's eyes. She grabbed the phone and placed it next to her ear. She could hear breathing on the other end.

"Shamiso?" Tanyaradzwa's gentle, husky voice rang out. There was no mistaking it.

Shamiso burst into jubilant sobs. Her mother nodded as she watched her. The lump melted away.

59

Tinotenda sat on the teacher's table in front of the class, as he always did, reading the paper. He had made it his mission to carry on the tradition of keeping everyone updated, in honor of Mr. Mpofu who had still not been found.

Tanyaradzwa and Shamiso sat next to each other, working out sums together. The new teacher walked in. She was a young, tall, dark woman with her hair pulled tightly into a bun. She seemed fresh out of university.

"Please get out your books," she said in a sharp voice. "You guys were making a lot of noise. Where is your class monitor?"

The class kept quiet. Shamiso glanced at Paida's seat. She had not returned. All they had heard was that her mother had moved her to another school, perhaps to avoid the humiliation.

"Okay, who can solve this for me?" the teacher asked as she scribbled a problem onto the board. The students remained silent. They had not covered this in class yet.

Shamiso smiled, remembering the book Mr. Mpofu had used to flood her with problems.

"I can," she called as she raised her hand in the air.

60

Her neck still itched. But as she held the cigarette in her hand, she could not help but wonder what it would feel like to find solace in something else. Perhaps music. Perhaps writing.

Shamiso stood backstage, listening to the crowd as they sang along to the band. She had never played in front of an audience before. She could feel the nerves setting in.

Tanyaradzwa emerged. "Are you ready?"

Shamiso nodded. Her heart danced a tango in her chest. The master of ceremonies announced their band. Shamiso breathed in deeply. The crowd cheered and the girls walked on stage.

She could see her mother and grandmother sitting in the front. Tanyaradzwa's parents were away to one side, under the trees. She glanced at Tinotenda in the back, standing with his saxophone in his hand, ready to whistle away. She signaled for the band to start.

The song began, instruments harmonizing gently and building into one voice, the band sending it into the air. The mbira led the tune "Ishe Komborera Africa." The slow, jazzy sounds of the saxophone danced on the horizon and provoked the keys of the guitar and keyboard.

Shamiso glanced over to Tanyaradzwa, whose rusty voice wove all the sounds together.

Heaven wept, touched by the melody. Shamiso's mother closed her eyes, face up, enjoying the drops as they kissed her skin. The crowd gloried in the wild, potent cries of the mbira as it bellowed and awakened a hope rare enough to amaze them and precious enough to allow an escape.

GLOSSARY

ambuya: grandmother

baba: father

chokwadi: honestly or truly

dhuku: headwrap

hadeda: a type of bird in sub-Saharan Africa. The name comes from the "haa-dee-daa" sound the bird makes when it is startled or feels threatened.

helper: in some parts of southern Africa, housemaids are referred to as helpers. This is considered a more polite name than housemaid.

Hondo Yeminda: the fight for land reformation in Zimbabwe in 2004. It was a movement to reclaim the land from white farmers.

"Ishe Komborera Africa": "God bless Africa." It is a popular song in southern Africa composed by a South African schoolteacher called Enoch Santonga. After Zimbabwe gained independence in 1980, the song was translated into Shona and changed to "Ishe Komborera Zimbabwe," the country's first national anthem.

jarcaranda: a subtropical tree with pale purple flowers that last a long time. This tree is common to the southern part of Africa.

GLOSSARY

kombi: a minibus used as public transport

mai: mother. It can also be used as a title (Mrs.).

maiguru: a term used to refer to an older aunt. This is the opposite of mainini.

mainini: literally translated as "younger mother." Used in Shona culture for a younger aunt or young ladies in general.

maputi: roasted maize corn

Mazoe: a concentrated drink produced specifically in Zimbabwe. Although the drink now comes in different flavors, the original and most popular flavor is orange.

mbira: an instrument found in most parts of Africa. Also referred to as the hand guitar.

mfana: kid

mukwasha: son-in-law. Also used in a more general way to refer to young men.

mwanangu: my child

sadza: a thick polenta-like maize porridge that is served with stew and vegetables. Sadza is the staple of Zimbabwe. It is also widely found across sub-Saharan Africa, but the name differs from country to country.

ACKNOWLEDGMENTS

I owe my deepest gratitude to a lot of my friends and family for encouraging me and supporting me through the whole writing process.

But firstly I would especially like to thank my good friend Janet Johnston, who has been like a second mother to me and who got me to publish this book. Thank you, among so many wonderful things, for literally playing agent for this book.

I would also like to thank my dearest friend and sister, Yeukaishe Hope Nyoni, after whom this book is named, for always being my designated reader and always telling me, all those years, to never give up and to keep hoping.

This book also would not have made it far without one of my loveliest friends, Kamogelo Chadi. I have never met anyone in my entire life who is so skilled at scaring procrastination out of a human being as she is. I owe you so much gratitude.

To my wonderful friends Keitumetse Teko, Tariro Mutya-vaviri and Nonjabulo Tabede, thank you for all the prayer and encouragement; thank you for basically always being my support system.

A huge thank you as well to my colleague Jean Moore, who took time out of an immensely busy schedule to read over earlier versions of this story and provide wonderful tips and criticism.

I also owe a lifetime of gratitude to my editor, Felicity Johnston, who accidentally discovered me and helped make Shamiso and Tanyaradzwa's story come alive. You are a true angel and probably one of the most patient people on this planet.

I would also like to thank Daniel Ehrenhaft, my brilliant editor at Soho Teen, who believed in this book as much as I did and helped bring Shamiso's story to life. And to the rest of the Soho Teen team including Rachel Kowal, Steven Tran, Alexa Wejko, Bronwen Hruska, and Janine Agro, who have worked so hard to make my dream come true. No words can ever truly express my gratitude, but I hope you all know how grateful I am for your hard work.

I must also thank the brilliant team at Bonnier Zaffre including Carla Hutchinson, Tina Mories, Talya Baker, Anna Morrison and Alex Allden for all the help and support, and for being very patient and extremely supportive to a new voice in YA fiction.

To my siblings, Tafadzwa and Heather Tavengerwei, Tendai Nyoni and Rejoice Gon'ora, thank you for being my back-up memory and helping me remember what 2008 was like when I forgot, and also for the many brilliant insights on what was happening in the country at that time. But thank you as well for always supporting and cheering me on.

ACKNOWLEDGMENTS

Another big thank you to my WTI-Moot family, Andre Apollus, Maria Bravo, Fuji Anrina, Jorge Seminario and the rest of my friends: Anvar Rahmetov, Elloa-Wade Saleh Aboubakar, Selma Matsinhe, Selma Boz and Kajori De. Thank you for all the food that was eaten in celebration of this book.

And of course, though this book is for you, Mom and Dad, thank you again for being you, and being so good at it!

Lastly, thank you to the many Zimbabweans whose stories of hope and perseverance during 2008 inspired this book. Never give up hope.